the Hunter's Prey

the hunter's prey

EROTIC TALES OF TEXAS VAMPIRES

Diane Whiteside

HEAT
NEW YORK, NY

THE BERKLEY PUBLISHING GROUP
Published by the Penguin Group
Penguin Group (USA) Inc.
375 Hudson Street, New York, New York 10014, USA
Penguin Group (Canada), 90 Eglinton Avenue East, Suite 700, Toronto, Ontario M4P 2Y3, Canada
(a division of Pearson Penguin Canada Inc.)
Penguin Books Ltd., 80 Strand, London WC2R 0RL, England
Penguin Group Ireland, 25 St. Stephen's Green, Dublin 2, Ireland (a division of Penguin Books Ltd.)
Penguin Group (Australia), 250 Camberwell Road, Camberwell, Victoria 3124, Australia
(a division of Pearson Australia Group Pty. Ltd.)
Penguin Books India Pvt. Ltd., 11 Community Centre, Panchsheel Park, New Delhi—110 017, India
Penguin Group (NZ), Cnr. Airborne and Rosedale Roads, Albany, Auckland 1310, New Zealand
(a division of Pearson New Zealand Ltd.)
Penguin Books (South Africa) (Pty.) Ltd., 24 Sturdee Avenue, Rosebank, Johannesburg 2196,
South Africa

Penguin Books Ltd., Registered Offices: 80 Strand, London WC2R 0RL, England

PRINTING HISTORY
Ellora's Cave e-book edition / 2001
Heat trade paperback edition / February 2006

Library of Congress Cataloging-in-Publication Data

Whiteside, Diane.
    The hunter's prey / by Diane Whiteside.—Heat trade pbk. ed.
        p. cm.
    ISBN 0-425-21035-9 (trade pbk.)
    1. Vampires—Fiction. 2. Texas—Fiction. I. Title.
    PS3623.H5848H86 2006
    913'.6—dc22   2005029144

PRINTED IN THE UNITED STATES OF AMERICA

10 9 8 7 6 5 4 3 2 1

For the three godmothers:

Ame,
the best psychiatrist ever seen by a character;

Julie,
the best friend any writer could hope to find; and

Brynda,
who wondered one day why there weren't
any vampires in Texas.

This one's for you.

the Hunter's Prey

la paloma blanca

a tale of
don rafael perez and ethan templeton

Dearest Pearl,

Thank you so much for your letter! It seems like an eternity since we vowed eternal friendship in Concord, outside Miss Amity's Young Ladies' Seminary. It has taken every ounce of strength that my sister, Cordelia, and I can muster just to survive this harsh Texas summer. We hope to return soon to Boston, if only we can obtain Father's permission. But he plans to remain here in Austin, searching for ways to help this rebel state return to the Union. I suspect he also hopes for ways to line his wallet, but he publicly speaks only of the good to be done here.

You ask if we have met any interesting young men. Most of the young men we meet are Army officers. Alas, Father will not permit us to do more than speak to men of the sword. He extended this ban to followers of Mr. Colt so very few men in this martially inclined dust hole are acceptable. Cordelia has been known to say that if we did not meet anyone soon, she would invent someone! However, we encountered two men last Saturday night who were very intriguing. I will tell you everything that I can remember of them.

Father had invited some acquaintances for dinner, which Cordelia and I attended as his hostesses. We were excused when the drinks were passed, a departure we both welcomed. The gentlemen here drink whisky and smoke the most appalling cigars all night long, whether or not there are ladies present! It is very distressing to both of us. In any event, Cordelia went directly upstairs to nurse her headache while I went to say a few words of thanks to the cook. (She had managed to provide a meal without beans, a most remarkable feat.)

When I went upstairs, I could hear voices from within our bedroom. It seemed that Cordelia was moaning, a most intense sound if somewhat low-pitched. I hesitated then approached softly, reluctant to disturb her if her headache had increased. Her moans did not sound pained so I went up to the door, holding my skirts so as to make the least sound. I put my ear to the door and heard words out of Cordelia's mouth. To my surprise, she was begging someone for more!

I could not imagine to whom Cordelia was speaking. This is a most uncouth town and she complains frequently of the lack of presentable callers. I crouched down and peered through the keyhole.

What should my stunned eyes behold but my sister, sitting on a man's lap! He was a tall blond man in a threadbare rebel uniform, seated on the edge of the bed, holding her arched across his arm. His hair spilled across her generous bosom so I could not quite make out all the details. He seemed to be kissing her throat and farther down. Her language was rather incoherent, but I am certain that she wanted more of whatever he was doing.

I observed them for some time. He had been able to unbutton the back of Cordelia's dress so that her underthings were very evident. His mouth was most busy, although I am not certain of all his actions since she spent much time clutching at his head. I believe his name was Ethan, since she frequently repeated that word. I blush to say that my hand reached under my skirts, echoing Ethan's movements.

Suddenly, I was picked up in a man's arms! I

squeaked with surprise as I beheld a giant holding me as if I were as light as a feather. (Which you know, Pearl, I am not!) He stood some inches over six feet, black hair and black eyes, olive skin, heavily muscled, a Roman nose, and a very nasty scar above one eye. He had quite the look of a conquistador from the days of Cortez.

"*La paloma blanca*," he murmured. "Little white dove, perched on the gallery to watch the excitement." He smiled at me, then kissed me. It was a very dream of a kiss, one to flutter any lady's pulse.

"Won't you invite me in, *mi paloma blanca*?" he asked. I could only nod yes as I stared at his mouth, hoping for more of his attentions. He lowered me slightly so that I could open the door, and in we went.

Ethan lifted his head as we came in but kept his hand busy on Cordelia. He did not seem surprised but simply lifted an eyebrow. Cordelia twisted her head around and glared at me. (Pearl, you at least must believe me. I was not spying on her so that I could inform Father! Cordelia has always accused me of such reprehensible behavior when, in truth, she is the one who ran to our patriarch with tales of my misdeeds. But she has not done that since this night's adventures so I have some hope for the future.) In any event, I mouthed an apology for interrupting her frolic and Cordelia soon went back to fondling Ethan's head.

"Continue as you were, Ethan," my gentleman said. "This young lady is desirous of seeing how a gentleman pleasures a woman. So make sure that you provide ample entertainment." Was I mistaken or was there the slightest emphasis on the word *gentleman*?

"As you wish, Don Rafael, but . . ." Here, Ethan hesitated as if seeking words. My gentleman fixed him with a stare that would have made even Andrew Johnson behave reasonably.

"Tonight is the first opportunity to see how well you have learned your lessons, Ethan. You know how to walk into a room and select your best prey from the adults present. You understand how to excite her passion, preferably by seduction but, if necessary, by blanketing her mind with lust. You have thus learned how to walk out of a room with any adult in it, your quarry full of carnal anticipation and more than willing to feed you. Now you must prove that you can dine discreetly, leaving your prey alive. You will not risk my family by killing, thereby making humans hunt us."

Ethan nodded, his eyes fixed on my gentleman, who continued the amazing lecture.

"Remember that feeding is better on emotion than on blood alone. You will answer to me if you forget that and harm either lady."

Ethan flinched as if he had been struck, yet Don

Rafael's voice had been low and even. I remembered how the officers had spoken to their men at the close of the late conflict. The slightest word had been attended as well as any minister's thundering sermon. Don Rafael's words held a similar grip on Ethan.

Don Rafael studied him for a moment before speaking again. "*Bien*. Now arrange yourself and the woman to provide the best display. My little white dove has known a man's passion before but now she wishes to watch. Is that not true, little one?"

I agreed, blushing hotly. How had he known of an occurrence that I had only told you, Pearl? Had he read my thoughts when I wished that drunken oaf had paid half as much attention to my rapture as Ethan was paying to Cordelia's?

Ethan bowed his head in acknowledgment then shifted Cordelia so she came astride him with her back against his breast, draped across his lap and her head arched back against his shoulder. He ran his hands over her and her dress slid away at his touch. He lifted her hips and soon stripped the obscuring cloth from her. My startled gaze beheld my sister's body attired only in a chemise, stockings, and her kid boots, outlined against a fully clothed man. Cordelia smiled at me in the exact manner she uses every Christmas when she gets to open her presents first as the eldest child. Ethan began to touch her in the most intimate fashion imaginable, paying considerable attention to her bosom. Cordelia's arms went up over her head, her eyes closed with a smirk, and she stretched, offering herself to him.

Don Rafael carried me over to the armchair and sat down. He settled me on his lap in a similar fashion, facing my sister and her lover. This left his hands free to unbutton my garments. I could not pay much attention to this state of undress as he simultaneously fondled me in a fashion comparable to that wrought upon Cordelia. His attentions were thorough but perhaps a bit absent-minded. He seemed more intent on how well Ethan displayed his education than on me, although I had no cause for complaint.

Ethan's hands began to center between Cordelia's legs. She twisted and thrashed against him in a most uninhibited manner. I could see every detail of her responses. His hands would move quickly then slowly, sometimes even more cautiously until they were still. Then an abrupt movement would bring such a gasp from her! He drove her up to the very brink of rapture and then kept her there for what seemed an eternity. (I confess that I writhed upon Don Rafael's lap as his hands took liberties with me during this time. My hands gripped his, seeking to guide him between my legs to where I knew release could be obtained. But he retained command of my carnal appetites and did not allow me to become so desperate as to stop watching my sister's burning desires.) I have never seen her lose all discipline as she did under Ethan's touch. She begged him for release, crying that he was cruel, cruel for torturing her in this way. (You would wish to be tortured in such a fashion too, Pearl!)

Ethan licked and sucked at Cordelia's neck, showing some very sharp teeth. She went very still once and Don Rafael growled. Ethan released Cordelia's throat immediately and then licked her. I could see a crimson drop sliding over her white breast as she sobbed again, begging him for still more.

Pearl, I do not know how Ethan could move his hand so rapidly between Cordelia's legs! Suddenly her entire body convulsed and she cried out. She arched against him, anchored only by his hand between her legs and his mouth on her neck. I could see him suckling at her, like a calf on a teat, as she screamed her pleasure. His body shuddered, contractions running through it in concert with the pull of his mouth on her throat.

"Ethan." Don Rafael's voice was scarcely more than a whisper but it cut like a knife. Ethan's head jerked as if slapped but he stopped pulling at Cordelia.

Finally she lay against him, a few slow ripples passing through her body. His eyes shut and he licked her neck slowly.

I burned to follow Cordelia over the precipice of delight. But Don Rafael had his legs firmly between mine and held my hands tightly, withholding any chance of completion from me. I was forced to sit there and study Cordelia's sated sleep. I cursed and fought him but his strength was too great. I demanded the same ecstasy that my sister had enjoyed! Pearl, he laughed at how little effect my struggles had! Then he kissed my hair, still chuckling, and quickly sought my intimate parts. I jerked in surprise at his acquiescence to my pleas but quickly fell into delight.

Truly, Pearl, I do not know what I was more distressed by at that moment: whether his first denial of my satisfaction or his casual and efficient provision of that pleasure!

I sat astride his legs, panting, and tried to recollect myself. I was intensely aware of the contrast between my moistly glowing body and the rough strength of the body supporting me. He did not seem unaffected by the passion that Ethan and Cordelia had displayed. In fact, I suspected that his masculine tool was pressed hard against me in hope of similar pastimes. But his discipline over himself was as great as the control he had exerted over me. He made no further movement but simply held me still as we watched Ethan and Cordelia's exhaustion.

Ethan opened his green-gold eyes finally and studied

me. His tongue slid out and cleaned the last drops of blood from his lips.

"May I watch you, Don Rafael?" he asked humbly.

Don Rafael chuckled and stroked the inside of my legs.

"*Bien*, Ethan, *muy bien*. Yes, it is time for this *paloma blanca* to coo. . . ."

Dearest Pearl, the most wonderful thing has happened! Reverend Smith has just stopped by. He is returning to Boston and will carry this letter directly to you. I know you will be intrigued by this tale, even half-written, so I must send this with him. I will send you the remainder as soon as I can write it.

Pray convey my love to your family. I miss you desperately and will write more to you soon.

But for now, I remain,
Ever your truest friend,

A—

Dearest Pearl,

I have found the ending of my previous letter! I will add but a few words to it so that I can send it off to you immediately.

I believe that the summer heat here is more oppressive than in Beelzebub's domain. Cordelia and I venture out only under protection of the evening's cool, except for Sabbath services, of course! While we have not met any new young men since my last letter (for there are few here worth meeting), at least we encounter them during times of frivolity and friendly congress at the dinners and dances that Father's friends offer. Then we retire to our room and read or dream of gallant men to bring excitement into our lives.

I believe that my last letter ended with me seated on Don Rafael's lap, looking at Ethan. Cordelia slumbered on the bed, so lost to dreams that she would not wake until the sun had almost finished its next day's course.

I am afraid to confess that I broke the silence with a question so unbelievable that even now, I blush to confess it.

"Are you vampires?" I asked, feeling a calm that owed much to my irritation at the gentleman holding me. I felt a slight ripple of surprise go through the big body holding me. Don Rafael tilted his head to look at me.

"We are, *querida*. But I give you my word: You have nothing to fear from us. We offer a simple exchange: rapture in return for a taste of blood. Our friends often find their way eased in matters outside the boudoir, as well. Your sister will awaken tomorrow, suffering only from the aftermath of pleasure and a slight lassitude. Her body will heal itself completely within a few weeks. She will remember nothing of this night."

Cordelia emitted a slight snore as he spoke, her usual sign of deep slumber. (As you well know, Pearl, her other sign is stealing all the covers but that is not likely to happen during a Texas summer!)

Don Rafael continued speaking in the most melodious tones for such a deep voice. "And you, *mi paloma blanca*, now have to concern yourself only with your own pleasure. You will sing like a dove tonight, I promise you, low and sweet, your voice quivering with ecstasy."

Somehow I believed him, Pearl! It truly was amazing that I accepted the assurances of this man, a vampire by his own admission! And yet I did trust him, at least for this much.

I must have relaxed in his hold because he slowly lowered his hand, bearing mine with it. My hands finished at my waist, grasped firmly by his strong fingers. I slanted my head back to look up at him for the first time.

"Will I remember this?" I asked. I yearned for memories to set against those of that drunken oaf who'd snatched my virginity away and then had the discourtesy to fall off a horse and break his neck before Father could bring him to account. (But enough of that old lament, Pearl. I must speak more of the gallant Don Rafael.)

Don Rafael arched one eyebrow in surprise but smiled at me. I was so close that I could see how that dreadful scar cut into him, even denting the bone above his eye.

"*Sí*, you will remember this," he granted me. "But you may only speak of this night's events once. And do not worry about Ethan. He is my servant and will do only what I command. *¿Comprende*, señorita?"

I nodded eagerly. You have so often yearned for adventure, Pearl, that I knew you would enjoy a tale of dashing men if I could but tell it.

Don Rafael kissed my cheek and then rubbed his against mine. It was a gesture of the most amazing gentleness and, yes, even friendship! I purred under it, enjoying the touch. He smelled like the finest of gentlemen's soap, sandalwood, I think. His teeth were excellent and his breath fresh and sweet. I thought suddenly that his kisses would be more pleasant than those from any of Father's guests downstairs.

"Ethan, convey the young lady to the chaise longue. Arrange her so that she may comfortably rest for the remainder of the night."

Ethan nodded in obedience and stood up. He carried Cordelia to the chaise and arranged her as directed.

All the while, Don Rafael kept me on his lap, murmuring into my ear. I am not entirely sure of what he said but some of it sounded familiar. Do you remember that Latin book your older brother had? The one that your parents refused to let us see but we spent an afternoon poring over? Don Rafael's words reminded me of those phrases, sweet nothings that a lover might whisper. My body softened at the liquid syllables and the light caresses of his fingers on my hands.

Ethan returned to stand in front of us, eyes lowered. I watched him idly while preening under my gentleman's touch.

"Curious, *mi paloma*?" Don Rafael whispered in my ear. "Would you like to see a man's secrets?"

My indolence fell away in a rush. As you well know, Pearl, curiosity is my besetting sin. I sat up straight and watched eagerly as Ethan slowly began to unbutton his gray jacket.

Ethan took his time removing his garments. I may be mistaken but it seemed that his every gesture was calculated to tempt a woman. I was almost shaking with excitement when he finally stood revealed in the lamplight. He was a splendid sight as he posed there, white as marble and clean muscled. His golden hair shone only as demure accents on his torso, not as a heavy pelt concealing his charms. My mouth watered at the sight of him, all ivory and gold. A tracery of thin silver lines covered his backside with one line crossing his breasts just above his nipples. (Perhaps they were scars from a whip or a knife. They did not seem to hinder him in any way.) I studied him, comparing him to what little I knew of men's bodies.

"What do you think now?" Don Rafael's warm breath caressed my ear.

"He is a fine figure of a man," I remarked, striving for savoir faire. "But he seems a bit," I hunted for words, "soft perhaps, between the legs. Your body doesn't feel soft there to me."

Don Rafael rocked with laughter. I blushed at my own words but chuckled with him. Ethan blushed too but continued to wait.

"Ah, *mi paloma*, what shall I do with you? So inexperienced and yet so observant! You are a delight! Ethan is very new to the feel of a woman's ardor as it flows through her blood over his tongue. He so far lost command of himself that he followed your sister into passion's release. Please accept our regrets that Ethan cannot yet offer you the full use of his manhood. He will take some time yet to regain himself after tasting your sister."

Am I mistaken, Pearl, or did Ethan's blush deepen at Don Rafael's words? But I did not dwell on Ethan's experience or lack thereof as Don Rafael continued speaking.

"Would you care to study another man's body? Mine is not so elegant as Ethan's but I can assure you that I am not soft between the legs."

I agreed quickly and soon was deposited on the bed. Ethan dropped to his knees next to the chair, watching Don Rafael but leaving him space to move about in.

Don Rafael divested himself of his garb, the typical attire for a Mexican gentleman here in Texas, without any seductive tricks. His short jacket and tight pants emphasized his intense masculinity. His movements' directness fired my blood so that my breath came faster and faster as his clothes fell away. He was a strongly built man, a veritable warhorse to Ethan's racehorse. Every muscle and sinew spoke of power while his hardness reared up between his legs with a stallion's vigor. (I must confess, Pearl, that I trembled at the size of his staff!) He had more than one brutal scar to emphasize a puissance that had been well tested by life. I was utterly conquered, as eager as any mare in season, before he even touched me.

He lifted my chin up with one finger and his mouth claimed mine. I was an eager pupil and our tongues soon twined and danced. . . .

I have few words for what passed next, Pearl. My

very senses were so dazzled that memory fails me. We kissed, oh how we kissed! And he caressed me with those magical hands, quickly freeing me of my few remaining items of clothing.

What more can I tell you? The feel of his mouth on my breast as he taught each nipple to beg for him? The slide of his long black hair across my hip as his lips moved below my breasts? Or the feel of his shoulders under my grasp, the muscles rippling as he moved? (His back was deeply scarred, like the former slave we saw at the abolitionists' rally. You would weep, Pearl, to see flesh and blood ruined so! And yet in that instant, I cared more for the raptures that body could bring me than its past torments.)

And his fingers, Pearl, oh such marvels they taught me! More than once I fell off the precipice of delight as his fingers and then his tongue played between my legs. Then his mouth traveled back up to my breasts and I clutched his head in my frenzy, twisting against him like a demented woman as we lay side by side.

Don Rafael said something softly, an order perhaps, but I paid little attention, too lost in passion to listen.

A gentle hand stroked my legs and I instinctively bent my leg to allow it freer access. The hand insinuated itself to where my desire raged hottest. I groaned in an ecstasy beyond all words as Don Rafael's hands and mouth ravished my breasts while Ethan stoked the fires below. Oh, Pearl, it was bliss beyond compare to have two men compelling me onward! I hope that one day you may feel the like of it!

My leg was urged upward until it at last clasped Don Rafael's hip. I rubbed him urgently, the prickle of his leg's hair a pleasant sensation for my sweaty thigh. We moved closer still and I felt his hardness pressing against me. This caused me to grow more excited yet. I gripped him fiercely with hands to his head, leg wrapped around his, and my head thrown back.

I begged him for more and he gave it to me. He entered me easily, sliding home on the liquid welcome my body rolled out for him. I felt utterly enveloped by him and yet marvelously free at the same time. Ethan caressed and licked us both, encouraging us to find our zenith. I sobbed my pleasure, my voice breaking slightly with each breath. My sounds were low and sweet, quavering like a dove's voice.

Don Rafael's lips sought my throat. I yielded instinctively and he rewarded me quickly. A fire blazed in my neck and I flew off my pinnacle into a storm of delight. Tremors racked my body as my blood flowed into his mouth on matching waves.

I must have lost consciousness then. I stirred once when horses went past under the window, perchance the end of Father's dinner party. But slumber returned quickly, held as I was in Don Rafael's strong arms, with Ethan lying on the other side of him. . . .

And that is the end of the tale, at least as much of it as I can now speak of. Cordelia and I both slept deeply on the following day, awakening to a few bruises and some lassitude. Cordelia remembers nothing of that evening's events, although I dare not speak of it directly to her. The small red marks on our necks were gone within a few days.

I hope to see Don Rafael again, perhaps in a few months when my body has recreated all of the blood he enjoyed so fiercely. But Father's business dealings have gone uncommonly well since that night. He speaks of-ten now of permitting us to return to Boston soon. Cordelia greets such talk with open delight while I strive to hide my uncertainties.

And so I conclude this letter, my dearest Pearl, in the hope that we will soon be reunited. Boston is my home and my future hopes are centered there. But I trust that you will understand if sometimes my fingers linger on my throat as I watch a full moon.

Your truest friend,
A—

sweet punishment

a tale of
don rafael perez and ethan templeton

Tomorrow I'll be wed for the second time. It's time to put away the past and look toward the future. So I'll write this story out, then burn it so I can find peace with the good man who returns my love.

My family was Irish, who fled to this country in hopes of finding easy money building the transcontinental railroad. Father could charm a bear from a honeycomb when he chose and my brothers inherited his knack. Unfortunately, they gained none of Mother's strong sense of honor and always avoided honest work.

So all too soon after our parents died, they were tricking folks out of their money.

To my young mind it seemed better than starving and I soon made a place for myself in their campaigns, as the specialist in entering dwellings by stealth to remove the more interesting contents.

It was simple enough for me to do back then. I was just as slender as I am now and could easily pass as a boy if I dressed in breeches, making it easy to pick a lock or climb up to an attic.

Then I met a young man in a similar line of work, Daniel Moynihan, a charming fellow whose knack with words was surpassed only by his brilliant blue eyes and deftness with the cards. Soon enough, we were married and traveling together. He died all too shortly: shot dead over a faro game.

I returned to my brothers and found them changed from my memory. They'd grown far too fond of the bottle and the dinner table, thus gaining bellies that strained every button. Their tempers had also increased, and I quickly learned to avoid crossing them at any cost.

It was a pleasant enough life otherwise. I met some interesting men who were more than willing to console a grieving widow for a night or a lifetime. I refused them all, still mourning for my beloved Daniel.

Only once did he not visit my thoughts when I studied a man. It was at an afternoon musicale where I found myself watching a big Spaniard with an aquiline nose and broad shoulders. And eyes like melted chocolate as he listened to the violins' song. A single glance from him would have coaxed me into the garden for a kiss without a second thought. But the invitation never came and I tried to forget my spell of womanly hunger.

My brothers now lived in Austin, a plain town with little to recommend it except its role as the capital of Texas. That made it the perfect locale for my brothers' current goal, which was to obtain a large piece of land as quickly as possible. Great tracts could be had then for a few forged bits of paper or a little gold handed to a judge. My brothers resented paying gold so they started hunting for land with a single owner. They reasoned it'd require fewer forgeries if only one person was named.

Soon enough they settled on the Santiago Trust as their target. A great mass of land did that trust hold, to say nothing of rich cedar forests, iron ores, and interests in much of the state's commerce. But try as they might, they couldn't discover who was the owner; only that many of the most respected men, and most feared too, were connected to the trust.

Finally, in anger and frustration, they demanded that I bring them the name of the real owner. I reminded them of the powerful men connected to the trust. My brothers took my warnings poorly and set about changing my mind. I agreed before more than bruises marked my body but resolved privately to leave them and Texas as quickly as possible.

So it was that I entered the First Bank of L— one evening. It had been solidly built to withstand Comanches and bank thieves and furnished in a rather stolid but luxurious style. A woman could have screamed herself hoarse without a soul noticing, once the iron shutters were closed. The arrangement of rooms was nothing remarkable but the large meeting room on the top floor offered a more elegant style than the other rooms.

I searched quickly but thoroughly, careful to leave no sign of my presence. While the bank was definitely linked to the Santiago Trust, it offered no clue as to the mysterious owner. Truth to tell, I was piqued that I couldn't answer that riddle since I'd always before managed to obtain whatever I wished. I did find an invitation to an evening meeting of the trust's friends.

My brothers weren't pleased by my lack of success but relaxed somewhat when I promised to spy on the meeting. In fact, they mellowed so much that they accepted an invitation to spend time in San Antonio drinking and whoring.

I dressed with great care that evening: black shirt, black wool trousers, and black boots. I braided my hair and pinned it tightly up under a black cap, such as a scruffy boy would wear. I didn't bother to bind my breasts; even my fond husband had called them "small and neat."

I arrived at the bank and soon gained entry through an upper window, which had been conveniently left open to gather cool breezes. A minute more saw me ensconced between rolled maps inside a large armoire placed in a corner of the big meeting room. I settled down to wait, certain that I could hear every word but couldn't be seen.

I watched some of the most important men in Austin, both Mexicans and Anglos, gather for the meeting. They chatted a little of trivialities, like the weather and the latest horse races, and avoided any taste of alcoholic spirits as they waited. Suddenly they fell silent as a carriage drew up outside and the new arrivals were greeted. I leaned forward, eager to see who could bring these powerful men to heel.

Two men entered, a tall Spaniard whose broad shoulders filled the doorway and a slender blond man, possessed of incredible beauty and the coldest eyes I have ever seen, following him. The Spaniard was striking, rather than handsome, with a brutally scarred face and eagle beak of a nose. I knew him immediately: Don Rafael Perez.

The same blaze of lust lashed through me as it had before. I cursed silently as I felt my nipples tighten. It would be difficult enough to eavesdrop without daydreaming about the bedroom potential of that big body.

Then I realized that the blond was Ethan Templeton, Perez's ramrod. A man whose name was spoken with fear and respect throughout Texas, a rough-hewn state that honored few. A chill brushed my excitement; if he found me, there was no telling what penalty he'd exact.

Templeton strolled around the room as Perez greeted the other guests. I quickly pulled away from the door so he wouldn't see me. My mouth was dry as a western river in the summer, and my heart pounded in my ears. But his footsteps moved away from the armoire as calmly as they had approached it, and I dared to look out again.

Suddenly a man's back blocked my view of the room. I bit my lip, swearing silently, as I recognized Templeton's fair hair. Surely he didn't know I was there. I was certain that I'd left no sign since I'd touched nothing in the room except the armoire.

When he didn't move, I relaxed slightly and strained to listen to the conversation beyond. Rustling papers and scraping chairs told me that the men had finally settled down.

Then the door flew open and a ruthless hand yanked

me from the armoire and into the room. I gasped in surprise and fought, using all the tricks from a lifetime outside the law, but to no avail. Templeton soon had me trapped in front of him, where none of my struggles loosened his tight grip.

Thankfully my cap remained on my head and I decided to continue my masquerade. Pretending to be a sexless boy seemed safer than considering the hard male body pressed against me and the growing ridge of masculinity that nudged the small of my back so relentlessly.

The guests surged to their feet at my abrupt arrival, startled and irritated.

"What the hell is that boy doing here?" demanded one.

"I'm afraid, gentlemen, that we seem to have discovered a spy," Perez drawled, strolling forward to stand in front of me. My heart beat triple time at the sight of that slow saunter, which reminded me of a mountain lion circling a deer.

"I'm sorry, Don Rafael," one man began but stopped when Perez lifted his hand.

"Enough said, Benjamin. I'm sure you checked this room most thoroughly. But sometimes mice can creep through the smallest cracks." His hand came down and lifted my chin. I glared at him fiercely, determined not to yield an inch. His eyebrow lifted slightly and his finger caressed my jaw contemplatively.

I caught my breath, startled by the contact, and looked into his eyes for the first time. His eyes were dark and cold and ancient, and held a considering spark deep within. I shivered involuntarily and heard Templeton chuckle quietly. He pulled me tighter against him so that his shaft nestled even closer. I tried to squirm away and his grip became brutally hard. I desisted with a gasp of pain and waited.

Mr. Perez's mouth quirked and he patted me on the shoulder before turning away.

"Gentlemen, I'm sorry but I'm afraid we must postpone this until we can be sure of being uninterrupted. I trust you won't mind joining your wives earlier than expected at the concert? *Bien*. My secretary will be in touch to reschedule our meeting." The men assented reluctantly and began to leave the room, most of them casting angry glances at me. No help there, not that I'd ever expected any.

Perez closed the door behind them then returned to stand in front of me. I swallowed, overwhelmingly conscious of being trapped between two big male animals.

"Was this your idea or your family's?" Perez asked.

"What are you talking about, Mr. Perez? Just let me go! I didn't hear anything," I protested.

"Your brothers' idea then," Perez remarked, his voice as icy calm as if he were ready to use a knife. I stared at

him and was glad he didn't speak my name in that tone.
"*Sí*, it's not hard to guess who would think of spying.
Fools who would rather gossip about iron ores than listen to a Mozart concerto." Dry amusement echoed as he
ran a finger down the front of my shirt and circled my
breast, hidden behind the shirt's linen. I choked as it
quickly swelled to meet his hand.

"Still, you must be punished," he mused, eyeing my
nipples as they surged against the rough cloth. "The true
question is, who should do the punishment? Myself since
you had the audacity to try to spy on me . . . or *sus her-
manos* because you failed to carry out their commands?"

My brothers? I cringed. "I, ah . . ."

"Ethan, how long do you think it would take to
properly lesson the lady?"

"A month, Don Rafael?"

Templeton's hand lifted my breast and squeezed it
gently, as if offering a fruit to Perez. Unbelievably, or
perhaps inevitably, it firmed more. I hissed slightly as he
plucked my nipple casually and it lengthened still further. I had no idea what I was going to do; I'd never felt
so helpless, or so sexually aroused.

"Excellent idea, Ethan. Tell me, señora. Whose punishment do you prefer to undergo? A month at our
hands or a lifetime with them?" Mr. Perez ran his finger
across my cheek. I closed my eyes until I could speak.

"If I underwent yours, wouldn't I also have to endure my brothers' after I left your domain?" I managed to say without looking at him.

"Very clever reasoning, señora," Mr. Perez purred as his touch glided down my throat. "Let me assure you that if you choose mine, then I would ensure that *los cretinos* would never lift a hand to you again."

My eyes flew to his face. I'd dance with the Devil himself for a promise like that.

"Never, señora," he emphasized, and his hand circled my throat lightly.

"Yours then, Mr. Perez," I croaked. I didn't know if he could keep his word but it was worth a try.

Both of Templeton's big hands now cupped my breasts, stretching the hidden nipples between blunt fingers.

"Are you certain?" Perez asked, and began to play with my shirt's top button. I barely managed not to moan as my body throbbed in rhythm with his touch.

"Yes, damn you!"

"A month should certainly be sufficient to teach you a few manners. The first lesson is that you shall always call me Don Rafael, not the Anglo Mr. Perez," he ordered as he undid the top fastening.

"Yes, Don Rafael." I choked, wondering what the hell I'd gotten myself into.

"Perhaps we should establish some rules for her stay," Ethan suggested, his voice a rich tenor next to Don Rafael's rumbling bass.

"An excellent idea, amigo. What do you have in mind?" A second button yielded to him, leaving much of my chest bare.

"She should have at least three orgasms before she is penetrated by anything larger than a finger or two," Ethan drawled calmly as his knee slipped between my legs.

I nearly fainted at the thought. More than one orgasm? I had a sudden vision of just how big Templeton's rod would be, once freed. Even so, it would probably be smaller than what rose behind Don Rafael's elegantly tailored trousers. My thighs tightened as a trickle of moisture glided down them from my overheated core.

"Three it is then," Don Rafael agreed, his eyes dancing. He rested his hands on my hips and lightly ran his thumbs up and down the buttons of my fly. My knees all but buckled. I know I swayed and was glad for Templeton's support.

Don Rafael's hand slipped down and cupped my mound through the thin cloth. I gasped helplessly as he rubbed me, encouraging cream to flow faster. Templeton kneaded my breasts and nuzzled my neck until my eyelids drooped.

"Tell me, amigo," Don Rafael purred as he used the seam's heavier cloth to rack me higher. "Since you set the trap for this little mouse, you shall have the first taste of her. Do you prefer her virginity or her blood?"

Virginity? "I'm no virgin," I spluttered, hauling my eyes open to stare at the man tempting me.

"Indeed, señora, but there are more virginities to a woman than the one guarding her womb. There is also the first time her throat welcomes a man's cock."

I blushed hotly at the memories his drawl evoked and he chuckled.

"And there is also the delight of her back passage," he went on in a deeper rasp. "Ah, the first time a woman is savored there, her channel like flame and velvet around the fortunate man's cock. And all the other delights of her body, her breasts, her pussy, and her sweet bud . . . all open and available to his hands. Her climax can be truly incredible then, overwhelming all of her senses."

I stared at him and reluctantly decided that he spoke the truth. Not for me, of course, but for a few other women somewhere. Neither Don Rafael's or Templeton's cocks could possibly fit inside me.

Templeton laughed softly and delicately bit my earlobe. I shivered, lust jolting down my spine from the touch. "Her blood, Don Rafael, if you please. A few drops only so she may serve us both tonight." Blood?

"You are generous, amigo! *Gracias*. You shall enjoy her blood and I will partake of her virginity." Don Rafael took his hand away from me and I bit my lip, determined not to beg for more of his touch. "Now, señora, we move on to the second lesson. You must be taught not to disturb others' privacy. Bend over the desk."

"What?" Templeton stepped away from me and I stared at the two men. "What the devil . . ."

"Now, señora." Don Rafael's voice was cold and bit like a knife. I remembered my brothers' idea of punishment and walked slowly to the desk in the corner. It was actually more of a small table except for the leather writing pad and writing instruments on top. Templeton lifted the inkwell and I bent over it reluctantly.

"Move back toward me, señora," Don Rafael instructed, his hands guiding me. "*Bien*. Now spread your legs wide. She is beautiful like this, is she not, amigo? Such sweet curves from this angle."

"Indeed, Don Rafael," Templeton rumbled, coming up beside the desk to study me.

"Wider still," Don Rafael murmured. "*Perfecto*."

I closed my eyes and waited for the first pain to hit me. Instead, Don Rafael stroked my ass and thighs. I trembled as he explored my nether lips through the wool, teaching them again to melt for him.

"You are damp, señora, but should be wetter still for the heat I want in you. A fire stoked by the drumbeat of my hand on your sweet ass."

I tried to tighten my legs around his hand and he chuckled and then gave a soft order in Spanish. I ignored that as I wiggled my hips in invitation and Templeton slipped under the desk.

Skilled fingers came to unbutton my fly. I jerked in surprise but Don Rafael's other hand came down to hold me in place. He caressed me again as more cream flowed from me. I moaned and wriggled and was vastly pleased when those damn trousers disappeared with a sudden rip.

Then Templeton began to stoke my fires. One hand played with my bud, teasing it so wickedly that I swear it doubled in size, while the other delved into my folds like a miner looking for the Mother Lode.

Don Rafael's first swat was light but echoed against my hunger, building my need for these men. I shuddered and sighed. The second swat was as light but deepened my lust further. I moaned again. "More," I muttered. "More."

The swats began to deepen. I didn't care: I wanted the orgasm that hung so tantalizingly close. If I could only get those male fingers to give it to me, to rub my bud harder, or probe into me further. I knew they could provide it and I began to beg shamelessly, my hips pushing back in desperation.

Don Rafael spanked me until I was burning with need, scarlet with hunger, aching for more of Templeton's enthralling touch. Fingers dwelt within me while others worked my bud into an aching knot. Cream gushed and ran down my leg. Still, they wouldn't let me come and I cursed them, begged them, then cursed again.

And I screamed like a Comanche war party when the hardest swat of all drove my bud down onto one blunt masculine finger and climax rocketed through every bone in my body. . . .

When I could think again, I was still lying across the desk, my shirt gone, while Templeton unbraided my hair. He combed it loose with his fingers and began to rub my scalp. I purred and leaned into his touch.

"Señora. Or shall I call you Catherine?" Don Rafael rumbled.

"Catherine's fine," I agreed before I saw what he held. It was an ivory wand, almost the length of my hand and cunningly carved into a series of bubbles and narrow valleys. He held it by its wide base as he calmly coated it with a thick layer of oil.

"Do you know what this is?"

I shook my head, still staring at the wand. It reminded me of a man's cock but what could it be used for?

"It is a dildo, of a style designed to awaken lust in the back channel."

"You're going to shove that thing into me?" I started to sit up but Templeton held me down effortlessly. I bucked briefly then quieted, still seething.

"It will ease my entrance into you, Catherine," Don Rafael remarked. "I am showing it to you now only so that you understand that we are men of our word. It would have been very simple to slip it into you while you lay stunned from ecstasy."

I flushed.

"It is no wider than two fingers, correct?" He stroked my ass with one hand as he displayed the dildo. I realized abruptly that a cooling lotion had been worked into my once-blazing skin. I still burned but it was tolerable, almost exciting.

"Yes," I whispered. I suddenly realized how much smaller the ivory was than either man's cock. My breath broke as lust whispered in my belly. "Please," I whispered, unsure what I asked for.

He smiled at me then and leaned down to kiss me. "You will find us stern but most enjoyable, Catherine."

"Yes," I murmured against his mouth. "Yes, indeed."

His mouth was more delicious than I'd hoped, and I

was panting again when he released me. "More, please." I sighed, turning my head to follow him.

"Ethan, amigo, display her. And distract her a bit, *por favor.*"

"Of course."

I squeaked as he gathered me effortlessly up into his arms. To my shock, he was naked to the waist, offering a tempting display of hot satiny muscles to lean against. I wriggled but he nuzzled my hair, then my temple and my cheek. I forgot my surprise and met his lips more than halfway. He kissed like a god, or an angel of seduction. More enticing than anyone I'd met except Don Rafael.

I barely noticed when he sat on the big conference table and murmured contentedly when he lay down on it. Indeed, I slid my hands into his hair and fell to kissing him long and deep, crouched over him like an eager tigress as he stroked my back.

It seemed perfection when he moved his attentions to my breasts. He suckled me hard, drawing me deep into his mouth as if I offered everything he found pleasurable. I arched for the moist heat of his caress and groaned when he worked my nipples into long aching berries.

And I shuddered in pleasure when two more hands played between my folds. My hips began to thrust, hungry to be ridden. A warm, rounded hardness circled against my backside and I pushed against it, blindly eager for more sensation, any sensation. It traced my rosebud again and again as Templeton suckled me, sending fiery trails down to my belly as others rose from the fingers tracing my bud.

I barely noticed when the wand entered me; I was too greedy for more of those masculine hands and that hard male mouth. In fact, I rocked so hard and long against those knowing hands, pleading for the climax I knew they could bring, that the wand's entire length traveled into me like a knife into butter.

I cursed like a mule driver when Templeton slid out from under me, ending my delicious climb before I'd reached the peak. I started to roll over and froze when the wand danced inside me. Muscles I'd never known trembled at the inner caress and tremors, almost of bliss, washed up my back and down my legs. I couldn't have sat up if Satan had nipped at my heels. "Oh, sweet heavens," I groaned and closed my eyes.

Don Rafael's chuckle crossed my ears, wicked and knowing. I blushed and tried again to move. He patted my ass gently and I trembled, startled by how his touch seemed to travel up the wand and into my spine. He tapped me again and again and the frisson slipped into my womb, evoking a wave of cream down my thigh. "*Excelente*, Catherine. You are more than ready to give Ethan what he has earned."

He scooped me up. I clung to him, too shaken by the ivory temptation inside me to argue immediately. He sat down in the big leather armchair before I could gather words and turned me so my back rested against him. Bare skin heated my back and crisp hair teased me, most of all where my derriere rested against him. . . . And his cock burned against my backside, reminding me of how my womb hadn't yet stretched for a man that night.

I shuddered and sank my fingers into his arms, laying my head back against his shoulder while I tried to think. But thoughts were beyond me when my body was so desperate for what it hadn't tasted in almost a year.

Don Rafael spread my legs further until his legs rested between mine. His fingers teased my bud until I moaned. I wiggled restlessly as my breasts ached and his chest hair teased my shoulders.

Then Templeton dropped in front of us and kissed my knee. He lifted my thighs and draped them over the chair's arms. Don Rafael aided him, opening me like a peach. Templeton began to lick and suck until I was as juicy as the fruit.

"Look up at me, Catherine."

"Why?" I grumbled but obeyed Don Rafael.

He smiled down at me, then deliberately curled his lip so I could see his teeth. Long teeth at the corners of his mouth.

Fangs? Was that what he'd meant by taking my blood?

Ethan's tongue circled my bud. I cursed fiercely. Their delay in giving me another climax was far more important than how they meant to enjoy themselves. "Damn you, hurry up!" I snarled and closed my eyes.

Don Rafael chuckled before his tongue bathed my neck again while Ethan hummed against my bud. I gasped when desire pummeled me harder, the wand teasing muscles and nerves into life that I'd never known before. I gushed more and more cream as they stoked me higher and higher, Don Rafael's hands on my breasts and belly while his mouth worked my neck. Ethan's fingers played a drumbeat of desire inside my core, stretching me while his mouth played games that tossed me into a frenzy.

I writhed on Don Rafael's lap, begging and moaning, half insane from the wand's dance in my backside, promising anything if they'd just finish me. And when I knew I couldn't bear any more, that I would die if I didn't reach climax soon, a rough thumb pressed hard on my bud as Templeton bit sharply into my thigh. The sharp pain became pleasure, more intense than anything I'd felt before. I shrieked as the climax tore out of me, racking me to the bone on a thunderclap of ecstasy.

The aftermath was still washing through me when Templeton's finger found me again. I gasped as a new wave built and crested when Don Rafael sank his teeth into my neck. I threw my head back, offering him any part of me he wanted, and screamed my pleasure like a mare in heat.

I lay sprawled across Don Rafael afterward, dragging air into my lungs like a colt who'd just run the Derby. I was well-pleasured as I'd never thought possible and yet . . . And yet . . .

Splendid as it had been, I wanted more. I wanted cock. I lusted for those large, hard, blazingly hot male organs still denied me. I needed to be filled and stretched until nothing existed but masculine strength driving into me.

I closed my eyes and tried to think of what to say. Thank you for punishing me? Certainly not, although I suspected that I might come to enjoy their style of retribution.

Thank you, kind sir? Not to someone who spanked that hard.

Thank you for pleasuring me but I want more? No, men whose eyes could become that frosty probably wouldn't appreciate requests from a burglar.

Then the damned ivory wand decided to jostle me again. I gasped as my ass clenched involuntarily, sending a cascade of lust into my womb. I groaned something incoherent, a plea for more or less of the torment, while I realized that they could easily stuff me with something larger than the ivory but just as unfeeling. Worst of all, they could probably make me enjoy it.

I was still pondering my options when Don Rafael stood up with a snort. I blinked, pushed my hair out of my face, and stared up at him. "What now?" I mumbled.

"Look at Ethan, Catherine," Don Rafael rumbled. "His cock demands satisfaction from a woman. Can you provide it?"

Templeton finished setting his trousers on the desk and turned to face me. I moaned greedily when I eyed his cock, a scarlet bar that curved just enough to kiss his belly. He sat down in the big leather armchair, fondling his cock in long slow pulls. A clear drop rose from the tip, then another in silent testimony to his potency.

I hissed my irritation at being so far away from it. Don Rafael set me down in front of the armchair. My mouth watered as I smelled the rich, musky scent of a man's lust.

I crawled forward the little bit necessary so I could rub my cheek against the handsome firebrand. He jerked slightly when I licked the tip, then caressed my head, playing with my hair. Encouraged, I began to explore it with my mouth and hands, old skills rising to guide me.

Soon he was moaning, long and low, as I worked more and more of him into my mouth and my fingers played with his fat balls behind their furry cloak. Lust rose in me and spiraled into my womb with every sound he made. My clit throbbed, desperate for attention, but I couldn't tear myself from him to satisfy it.

As I bent over him so I could swallow him deeper, a strong hand slid up the inside of my thighs. I willingly came up onto my knees, humming as my nose brushed his masculine fur. Templeton's hands tightened in my hair, then gentled into a slow pull and release that matched the rhythm of my mouth on his cock.

And thank heavens, Don Rafael's hand began to tease and tempt my clit. I groaned and spread my legs wide, wagging my hips in invitation. I cared nothing for what either man thought, or why they were there, just so long as they gave me what I hungered for.

The ivory wand slipped out, to be replaced by two fingers. I pushed back on them, aching for something bigger and hotter and harder. A chuckle, a few soft words in Spanish and three fingers entered me, stretching me wide. Four fingers widened me and I writhed. I'd have screamed my demands like a fishwife except that Templeton tasted too good to leave.

A blunt tip glided up through my folds and teased my backside. I shuddered in longing for more . . . and it slipped in. Just the tip, mind, but that was enough. I froze in shock, then his finger teased me again. I groaned as the sweet tremor flashed through my hips. His cock began to move again, every inch marked by another skillful stroke to my clit or through my nether lips.

Frankly, I'm not sure I needed those attentions. I was so eager for cock that the slow, hot ache as he filled me felt like the prelude to heaven.

He paused when he was buried to the hilt in my ass. Only the tip of Templeton's cock rested in my mouth now as a long shudder ran through me. And I wanted more. I needed to be the woman who held everything these two strong Texas men could give her.

Don Rafael said something harsh and urgent in Spanish. He started to ride me, long and slow at first while encouraging my clit, then deeper and faster as I responded. Templeton gripped my head and began to fuck my throat in an answering rhythm. Fire blazed up and down my body, from my deepest core through my backbone and out through my skin, until I was a bonfire waiting only for the torch. They tunneled deeper into me, their thrusts seeming to meet at my heart. Nothing existed for me except the two stallions filling me.

Climax came closer, closer . . . I pushed harder and harder into the two men until suddenly, I came. A scintillating pinwheel of sparks blazed before my eyes as wave after wave roared through me. I was dimly conscious of first Templeton, then Don Rafael's climaxing into me.

I think I smiled. I know I fell asleep without opening my eyes. And afterward . . .

I began my stay as only a month's diversion for them but they taught me how to look toward tomorrow, not yesterday, while finding joy in the present. They rescued me from my brothers and gave me a fresh start in Colorado afterward. More reward than a cat burglar deserved and the sweetest punishment a woman could hope for.

May they find as bright a future as they gave me.

champagne cocktail

a tale of ethan templeton with mention of don rafael perez and jean-marie st. just

Bartender! I'll have another one of your champagne cocktails, please.

How many have I had so far? Does it really matter?

You sure do know how to make a real champagne cocktail. Sugar cube soaked in bitters, then champagne, finally brandy. Of course, you do need a really excellent French brandy to top it off. It's a drink that's a lot like life, don't you think?

Thank you, young man. What a lovely night this is, sitting here looking out at the moonlight on the ocean, with a good drink and a handsome man close by.

Did you tell me what your name is? John? That's a lovely name. Did I mention I have a fellow named Johnny? Of course, he's a much older man than you are. Johnny has a waistline that a girl can't hardly put her arms around.

But he's definitely good for a lot of banging, if you know what I mean. His tongue knows how to take a girl to the stars, too. I've spent many an hour, writhing and yowling like a cat in heat, while Johnny worked that magic.

Johnny always knew how to treat a girl right. He loved to give me presents, expensive presents like a fur coat and fancy silk underthings. He used to give me cash too, lots of beautiful money to go shopping with. Sometimes I'd just take some money for myself and have a fine time shopping.

If Johnny knew I'd taken the money, he never said anything. He'd just rub my rear so that my underthings rode high, letting his hand in. His fingers would go to work until I grabbed anything nearby for balance. He always liked to hear me ask him for more.

Champagne was my drink then. It had to be champagne, bubbling and bright as my mood. Johnny bought me my first champagne cocktail on the night we met.

I can tell that you know how to treat a girl right, too. The way you pour that champagne out of the bottle so that the bubbles foam up in the glass . . . Mmm, that must draw the ladies like flies to honey.

Oh yes, I had a lot of fun with Johnny. He had a speakeasy back when those places were highly sought. It was the finest speakeasy in Austin. He let me decorate it just the way I wanted. So I got a fancy decorator from New York City and we did it up first-class: gold and mirrors, with bright lights and straight lines. They called the style Art Deco and I thought it looked just as elegant as that fancy French king's palace.

Everything in it was the best that money could buy. Johnny would even bring in pricey wines and liquors from New Orleans. He always said he wanted to make Texas proud of his place. All the high-class people came there regularly, including the chief of police.

Of course, lots of people were resentful of Johnny. They kept trying to cause trouble for him. So Johnny just had to keep a bunch of young men around to head off trouble. Fine young men too, muscled and fast with their guns . . .

Did I mention their weapons? Well, I made sure that those young men had good weapons—other than what Mr. Colt provided. You see, Johnny couldn't always come through for a girl, if you know what I mean. But he really enjoyed watching me with someone else. Of course, what he really preferred was seeing me with other women.

But I, well, I like the feel of a big dick pushing up into me, pardon my language. There's just something about the feel of a man sweating and straining away as he pounds between your legs. It's a pulse that's always sent shivers up my spine. . . .

Where was I? Oh yes, Johnny's young men. Well, Johnny and I worked out an arrangement. He got to see me from time to time with young women. But I got to audition all his young toughs for display in his bed. I made sure that, if and when Johnny ever wanted to see me being well-ridden, there was a young man handy who was ready, willing, and able to perform. Such lovely boys they were too.

I had to ask Johnny's permission first, of course. He called me his Theda Bara, for all the young men crowding around me. I liked the sound of that and tried to live up to the name. I dressed like a vamp, and I had fun like a vamp. Isn't it crazy, the things you do when you're young?

One day, Johnny started having trouble with another speakeasy owner. Police raids had always been just a nuisance before, but now the police started coming by all the time and even destroying things. I lost a fine set of champagne flutes once. It was dreadful.

So of course, Johnny's friends made sure that the police treated the other man's place similarly. Matters

became more exciting when the young toughs were involved. One time, some of Johnny's young men even
sprayed the other speakeasy with gunfire, and a handful
of guys were killed too.

Once, the other owner sent a few boys past Johnny's
place to shoot things up. A truck was delivering some
wine at the time, and both the driver and all his stock
were lost in the gunplay. The street was red for days until the next hard rain.

Johnny took me out for dinner at a fine steak house
to get my mind off that bloody street. The restaurant
was famous for the best steaks in Texas but it looked
very old-fashioned with its dark woods and scarlet
drapes. It even had steer horns on the walls.

They seated us in one of the private rooms, so everyone could pretend that we weren't going to drink alcohol. Johnny ordered his usual fancy French wine.
(You'd know about expensive wines, wouldn't you,
sugar?) But the waiter said they didn't have any of that
vintage. Johnny got angry and started fuming. He just
wasn't used to anyone saying no to him. Why, his face
even turned red.

The waiter called in a fancy Frenchman, tall and well-
dressed, with blue eyes and light brown hair. I didn't
pay much attention to him because I was watching
Johnny. I could see that Johnny wasn't paying much

heed either to all the Frenchie's talk of other wines. Johnny just kept getting louder and louder as he demanded the wine he always ordered.

The commotion brought another man over. The waiter really snapped to attention at his arrival and called him Don Rafael. Don Rafael explained that his supplier had lost a deliveryman in the current troubles, the same deliveryman who had died outside Johnny's place.

Well, Johnny didn't like this explanation but Don Rafael and I worked together to quiet him down. Don Rafael was a big Spaniard—taller than any other Spaniard I'd ever seen. He had black hair and black eyes, like most Spaniards, and his nose hooked like an eagle's beak. With that nasty scar over one eye, he didn't look the type to get ruffled by the loss of a wine shipment. His calm helped settle Johnny down.

Finally Johnny let himself be bribed by the promise of a special show, featuring me and one of the hat-check girls back at the speakeasy. Don Rafael treated us to some fine brandy before we drove back to Austin. I always drank fine brandy after dinner with Johnny. . . .

Thank you, sugar. A new cocktail tastes really good right now. I haven't thought of that dinner in years. I've never spoken of it before, even to Johnny.

It was right after that when the drifter showed up. Johnny had put out the word in Dallas and Kansas City that he was looking to hire. A number of young toughs showed up but most of them weren't worth the time of day. So Johnny and I would both audition them and then let them go.

But this fellow was different. Tall and slender, with blond hair and hazel eyes, he moved like a wildcat. All quiet-like and very dangerous. You knew that this one had killed before. That his crotch was well-filled-out was an added bonus to my way of thinking.

He sat down at the bar, just sipping on a whisky and watching the room. Our fellows noticed him immediately and passed the word to Johnny. One of the cigarette girls mentioned him to me when I was freshening up after a quickie with the bouncer. Of course, I went out to see the drifter too.

I perched myself next to him at the bar and tried to talk to him. He looked me over and seemed to see all of me, right down to my brand of French underthings. I know he could see that my dress hem didn't quite reach the top of my stockings. (I've always enjoyed seeing a man's response to my legs. They're good, don't you think?)

But he didn't react like men always did to me. He told me that I wasn't worth the effort needed to screw me. Can you imagine? No man had ever turned down an invitation from me. The North Pole was warmer than his eyes when he went back to his drink.

I was sure that I could change his mind if I just worked hard enough. I talked to him some more, sipping my champagne cocktail and leaning close. But he always kept a distance between us. I stroked his arm and felt the muscles under his sleeve. He moved his arm away and I could have cursed.

One of the guys came out and asked the drifter upstairs to talk to Johnny. He stood up right away for that invitation. I followed along behind, watching that smooth walk. He strolled as confidently as a gunfighter moving down a cow town's main street. He truly had the finest ass I have ever seen on a man.

He shook hands with Johnny in the office and they looked each other over. Something passed between them and Johnny told me to leave. I started to protest but Johnny insisted. I let him get away with it this time, because he didn't seem quite himself. A little distracted maybe. I went back to the bar and tried to amuse myself by looking at all the men there. I couldn't imagine any of them with a better weapon than that new fellow though.

Finally, Johnny summoned all his men upstairs, and I went too. Johnny was waiting in his office with the new guy over by the window. Johnny had a spot of blood on his collar. It seemed odd to me because he didn't need to shave more than once a day.

He introduced the new fellow as Ethan and said he'd be joining the gang. Ethan was good with a gun and would be doing some special work. We all knew what that meant—the undertaker would be doing cleanup after the special work.

Some of the fellows were pleased because they wouldn't have to do the killing. But most of them were just plain frightened. I just became hotter for Ethan, even though I was a little scared.

I talked to Johnny later that night about me and Ethan putting on a special performance for him. I waited until he was content and sleepy after a really good fuck before I asked him. I was curled up against him, the way he liked me. Boneless as I always was after Johnny's brand of starting things off before finishing with a roar.

Johnny said that Ethan would be the best judge of whether or not he would perform with me. But until Ethan asked me, I wasn't supposed to bother him. That angered me but Johnny wouldn't listen to any of my arguments. Finally, I had to drop the subject.

Johnny's refusal didn't stop me from watching Ethan every chance I got. I knew every detail of him, from the way he walked to the way he smelled. He looked so good under the electric lights in the speakeasy, and I daydreamed about how he'd look in my bed, that blond hair lit by the early morning sun . . .

You'd stretch out fine in bed, wouldn't you, sugar, for a beautiful woman? A woman hot and eager for you? A woman can just tell when a man knows how to pour himself into his lady like he pours a drink. I know you can do that, sugar; I've been sitting here watching you mix drinks. . . .

Thank you, sugar, for the fresh drink. Fine alcohol served by an expert makes it a real pleasure to sit here chatting. Just talking about what happened so long ago . . .

Johnny started acting funny about money matters shortly after that. He'd never cared much about money before; he'd just said that it was mostly for keeping score and spending on pretty ladies. Now he had all the books brought to his office and started reading them at all hours of the day and night. I'd catch him sometimes with the books laid out on the table while he talked to Ethan.

I tried to distract him. I paraded in silks straight from Paris and writhed under his hands and tongue until my voice was hoarse. I sucked him off more than once, surrounded by ledger books.

But nothing worked. Johnny's bookkeeper even got concerned that Johnny didn't trust him. Johnny reassured him about that and the bookkeeper relaxed a bit. But the books stayed in Johnny's office, close to him at all times. I kept wondering why Johnny was fussing about things that had never mattered to him before . . .

Do you ever find yourself doing that, sugar? Suddenly just polishing a part of the bar that no one can see? That no one can get to? Just to have something to do. Maybe it was only nerves on Johnny's part. But he'd never been nervous before . . .

Johnny's chief lieutenant, Hickok, didn't like Ethan at all. He muttered on and on about how no one knew Ethan and how Ethan could be doing all sorts of nasty things during the daytime, especially since Ethan only showed up after dark. He kept trying to pick fights with Ethan. But Ethan would just look at him in that cold way and move on. I figured the problem was that Hickok was simply drunk and jealous of the time Johnny spent with Ethan.

One night, Hickok had even more whisky in him than usual. I heard him come upstairs, hitting his hands against the wall. (You ever seen a man do that when he's too drunk to stand upright without help? Walks down the hall, thumping the walls every step just to make sure he knows which way is up.) A big heavy guy like Hickok—well, it almost sounded like a hammer.

I was in my room, trying on a new dress in hopes of getting some attention out of Ethan. I came out right away to stop Hickok before he bothered Johnny. But I found the oddest sight in the hallway.

There was Hickok in Ethan's arms. It looked like Ethan was kissing him on the neck, and I stopped dead. I burned with envy, feverish to have Ethan's arms around me. I felt my whole body clench with lust.

Then the men shifted slightly and I could see more. Hickok had his eyes shut, with a horrified look on his face. He wasn't fighting though. I hesitated, not sure what to do.

Ethan's eyes opened and he stared at me. I could see a little blood on his lip. I knew then and there that I had interrupted something that was none of my business.

I blinked and popped back into my room, mumbling something about being sorry to disturb them. The last thing I saw was Ethan watching me with his mouth still fastened to Hickok's neck. It almost looked like he was sucking on Hickok, but surely that couldn't be.

Do you go to the cinema often, sugar? I always have. Now I've seen a lot of things in the movies, from vampires to King Kong. But those were made-up stories about monsters, not real-life. This was real. A man's teeth on another man's body. It still shakes me up to think of it. . . .

Yes, thank you. A drink tastes real good after remembering that sight.

What happened to Hickok? Did he sober up? Would you, a bartender, want a good customer to stop drinking?

I wish he had though.

I heard the next morning that they'd found Hickok dead in an alley off Guadeloupe. He'd been filled with bullets and there wasn't much left of him. Funny thing though, the newspaper photos didn't show any blood around the body. But maybe the newspaper prettied up the photo some to make it acceptable for family viewing.

Johnny got angry, said the other gang was responsible for Hickok's death. Ethan never said anything about seeing Hickok that night and I wondered if I'd really seen anything. I went to church though, for the first time in years, and said a prayer for Hickok. . . .

Thank you, sugar. I needed another drink. I've been drinking champagne cocktails since I was sixteen. You make a very good one and it takes me right back. . . .

The fellows were more nervous after Hickok's death. The men walked around each other like bantam roosters just looking for a chance to strike at the other gang.

I couldn't help myself. No matter how much I sweated and sobbed in Johnny's bed, no matter what I'd seen or not seen, no matter how much death seemed to be walking the halls, I kept watching Ethan, begging him with my eyes for an opportunity to get closer. I was half-scared he would touch me and half-scared that he wouldn't. It was like chewing the sugar cube at the bottom of a champagne cocktail: sweet and bitter at the same time.

I can still see him sometimes when I close my eyes. Those green eyes studying the gamblers and the drunks, like a rattler watching mice.

One night, just after sundown, I went outside for a smoke on the rooftop. One of the fellows was keeping watch there but I told him to go away. I wanted some time alone to think about Ethan, try to talk myself out of hungering for him, tell myself again that I only dreamed about him because I couldn't have him.

The fellow argued with me a bit. He said that something could happen. There'd been talk that the law would raid this joint. It was his job to protect Johnny's place.

I told him that I'd keep an eye out. If anything happened, I'd sound the alarm.

He left finally. Reluctantly but he left.

Heaven help me but I forgot about keeping watch before the door closed behind him. It was easier to picture Ethan in my bed.

So I stood up there, looking out across the alleys and rooftops in the last rays of light. Of course, I started thinking about all the possibilities of that cruel mouth

of his. And his hands—slender but fast and deft. Or that
beautiful ass . . .

Suddenly a hand slid up my throat and pulled me
back against a man. I jerked and fought but the man's
other hand slid down my breast. He nipped my earlobe
and then my neck below it. I froze when I recognized
Ethan's touch from my dreams.

He muttered in my hair that maybe, this time, I was
worth the effort. I tried to turn so I could slap him for
that but he kept me tight against him.

He caressed my breast insolently and I began to
tremble against him. Every movement roused me still
higher until I was writhing against him.

I closed my eyes to enjoy the feeling. But he growled
in my ear to keep my eyes open and watch the city, look
at the streets. I pleaded that I couldn't pay attention to
buildings while he touched me like that. His hands went
still and I knew that he wouldn't fondle me again unless
I looked out at those piles of brick.

I opened my eyes and he stroked me again. I blinked
and then gasped when he ran his hand up my leg. So I
stared out at the city, eyes wide and moaning his name,
as he worked me over.

Suddenly a string of police cars pulled up the alley
and surrounded the speakeasy. I opened my mouth to

scream a warning to Johnny but Ethan's teeth bit hard into my neck. Climax struck me like a bullet just as I realized how my blind hunger had betrayed my dear Johnny. . . .

Give me another drink, will you, sugar? Some French brandy, please. I need to wash away that memory.

The cops arrested Johnny and his fellows then turned them over to the IRS for tax evasion. Taxes, can you imagine that? Well, if it was good enough to put Capone away, I guess it was good enough for Johnny.

There was blood on my neck when the cops found me on the roof. They hustled me out of there to the hospital so a doctor could take a look. Actually I think they just wanted me out of the way.

The last thing I saw before getting into the ambulance was Ethan standing with two other men, just beyond the cops rushing around like roaches. He was with the steak house's owner and that wine waiter, the big Spaniard and the Frenchman.

Ethan treated the big Spaniard with a reverence that he'd never shown Johnny. I knew that he'd come to the speakeasy because that man wanted him to. Maybe for the money to be gained from taking over the speakeasy but maybe not. I never heard talk of any big Spaniards running a fine speakeasy, then or later. Maybe the Spaniard just wanted a more peaceful town.

I felt so sick then that I was glad to be heading for the hospital. I swore that I would never be disloyal to Johnny again, in any way . . .

The newspapers were full of talk for weeks about all of the speakeasies being shut down and their owners hauled off to jail. When things quieted down, speakeasies started opening up again with new owners. Wild Bill, Hickok's younger brother, bought Johnny's place and reopened it. The new owners were very careful to keep things quiet and avoid attention from the cops.

Johnny spent ten years in the Big House before his heart got him out of there. We got married on his first day of freedom. See my ring? Big diamond, isn't it? Johnny always did know how to treat a girl right.

I saw Ethan again right after Johnny got out. He was standing under a streetlight, flipping a coin. It had been ten years but he didn't look a day older, still young and sexy as sin.

As soon as I saw him, I turned around and went the other way as quick as I could. I couldn't bear to look at him and remember what he had made me watch. Then I talked Johnny into moving someplace far away. That wasn't too hard to do. Speakeasies weren't the same after Prohibition ended and he felt like taking things easy after the Big House.

Now we live down here in Florida where the

weather's always warm. We play gin to pass the time, and sometimes we'll play canasta with friends. Or we'll walk on the beach.

Johnny still talks about the shows I used to put on for him with other girls. He even teases me about looking at other fellows. I don't do anything more than look now. I haven't asked permission to be with another man since the night they arrested him.

But mostly Johnny and I just hold hands. It's what he's best at doing these days. . . .

I drink brandy now if I drink anything. But sometimes I feel the need to remember the past. Then I go out and find a good champagne cocktail, to relive the days when I was young and bubbly as the wine.

Thanks for listening to me, sugar. You're a very kind man to listen to the ramblings of an old lady. I sure do appreciate the offer of a taxi.

I'd better be going now before Johnny wakes up from his nap.

the great chicken roost

a tale of jean-marie st. just

Okay, Mary, I'll tell you the story. You've heard parts of it before and I guess it's time to tell you the whole truth, now that you've turned twenty-five. You're married with a baby on the way so I think you can understand. And we've talked about some very racy things before.

Besides, it's better than watching for news about Korea, even if your husband isn't in the Army and my husband is retired. But I can only tell it just this one time, because I promised him then. If you ask any questions later, I'll have to say that I can't answer you.

I was wild when I was growing up but usually a good girl. I'd do some things like ride my pony down the town's board sidewalks. Heck, all the boys pulled tricks like that too back then. But nobody expected a girl to do crazy stunts, and I wound up with a reputation for being willing to do anything.

My parents weren't much help since they put most of their attention on working hard. All of us nine children were expected to do our chores and stay out of trouble, without requiring much attention from them.

One night, the local preacher's son and I played a game of double dare in the graveyard. He won—if you can call it that—and you were conceived that night. Of course, he denied everything, my parents wouldn't speak my name, and I went to Aunt Mabel's in San Antonio to have you.

You've heard all of this before but I still like to talk about it. I loved you from the minute you were born and couldn't give you up. All those black curls on your head, those big blue eyes, and your perfect little fingers. I thought you were the most beautiful baby in the world.

Aunt Mabel understood and she offered to raise you, if I could get some money to help out. Times were tough then, with the wind constantly blowing and the dust swallowing up houses and farms and towns too.

I tried to find respectable work but couldn't. Finally,

I ended up at Miss Jessie's place, where I worked as a boarder. That's what the working girls were called: boarders.

It was pretty simple work, especially once you and the client were alone in the bedroom. Just fifteen minutes to negotiate price, pay, undress, and do the act. Only the missionary position was permitted and Miss Jessie would wallop any client she caught trying some of that "foreign" nonsense. She was a slip of a thing, no taller than you were at thirteen. But every man paid attention when she swung that thin iron bar.

Yes, "foreign" included anything involving the tongue on any portion of the boarder—or the client. The boarder couldn't be on top of the client, or . . . I'm sure you get the idea.

You're giggling, Mary. Well, so did I, after I learned better.

Miss Jessie's rules of conduct for the boarders were actually a lot harder to live by. But she was fair and she spelled out all of her rules in a proclamation posted in the kitchen, where everyone could see it regularly. There were rules for receiving callers too, Miss Jessie's name for a man that a boarder saw regularly outside of a business relationship.

I visited you and Aunt Mabel to celebrate your first birthday. But it was after ten that Saturday night, thanks to the bus breaking down twice, when I got off in Susanville.

It had been a hot day and was turning out to be a hotter night, unless a thunderstorm came along to cool things off.

Susanville was a little town then and worse hit than most by the hard times. San Leandro, the next town west, was doing better. Of course, it had Rafael Perez and the Santiago Trust, rather than a mayor who claimed a personal chunk of every nickel.

Scientists had found ancient animal tracks in Susanville, made millions of year ago. Rich Eastern folks wanted to dig those rocks up and take them home. The locals thought the rocks had been sent from heaven to give them jobs. The mayor believed the rocks were there to make him rich, and he was making sure that no rock left Susanville until coins clinked in his pocket.

I started walking to Miss Jessie's as soon as I got off the bus. Miss Jessie's rules said boarders had to be back by six in the evening and I was late. Her place was just outside town and next to the highway. It was so near that folks passed it every Sunday on their way to church.

I stayed close to the buildings, trying to keep in the light from inside. I had just paused under an awning before crossing the street when three men came out of the saloon behind me: Mayor Jones, his crony Bixby, and a stranger.

The stranger was a tall man, dressed beautifully in a linen suit, good boots, and a snappy Panama hat. He looked cool and calm, as if he'd never raise a sweat, no matter what the weather or companion. He was handsome, with deep blue eyes, brown hair, and clear skin, and appeared more of a gentleman than anyone I'd ever met. He seemed young too, perhaps twenty-five, until I saw his eyes. They were weary with a knowledge born of experience and grief. I wondered if he was a bootlegger who hoped to join one of the mayor's rackets.

The mayor was a big man who liked to pretend that he still had the trim figure of forty years ago. He always dressed a little too well and sweated continuously in hot weather.

Bixby had followed Jones since grammar school. He stood taller than the mayor and was rail thin. But he was so mean and nasty that he never had to explain twice to anyone what the mayor meant.

The mayor told the stranger, using some very impolite language, that the rocks could stay in the ground for another million years for all he cared. He'd take his money first, before giving permission to dig up those rocks.

The gentleman was unmoved by the mayor's ranting and waited him out. He looked a bit regretful at the mayor's language but not angry.

"You'll give permission tonight, Mr. Jones, or you'll regret it." He had a lovely voice, with the slightest hint of France, which made me want to sit down and listen.

"What are you going to do to me? You're just a fancy lawyer for the Santiago Trust with no say in what goes on here. This is my town and I say there's no digging until I'm happy. You understand?"

"I understand that Susanville will have another mayor within a week."

I shivered at his tone of voice. I'd heard threats before but only from drunkards and fools. His words were a promise that chilled the air.

The mayor was shocked for a moment and then he sneered. "Never happen, not in my town."

The gentleman shrugged slightly. "We'll see."

"What're you doing out this late, Annie?" Bixby smelled like cheap whisky as he leaned down to talk to me. I flinched, wishing I had kept going instead of looking at the stranger. Bixby was a regular at Miss Jessie's and every girl tried to evade her turn with him.

"Heading to work, Mr. Bixby." I stayed put, knowing from hard experience just how much he liked women who ran.

"Well, now, isn't that fine? I was just heading that way myself."

I tried to think of something to say but my mind kept picturing me seated in a car next to Bixby. Then the stranger's voice sliced into the silence.

"The lady is traveling with me."

Bixby laughed as he spun to face the stranger but fell silent under the stranger's glare.

"If you wish to be useful, Bixby, you may put the lady's suitcase into my car. After that, I'm sure that you and Mr. Jones have business elsewhere."

My eyes widened as Bixby meekly took my suitcase and carried it to a beautiful Packard parked next to us. I couldn't have said anything to save my life. The mayor snarled something that began with a string of unrepeatable syllables and the stranger spun on him.

"You will respect this lady's presence, Mr. Jones, or you will be silent. Do you understand?"

Mayor Jones spat tobacco juice and sneered. "You're a fool for treating her like a lady when she's available to any man who can find a chicken to pay with."

He started to say more but suddenly stopped and clutched his throat. I stared at him and then at the stranger, who was studying the mayor regretfully, as if saddened by the mayor's words.

"Since you have nothing of consequence to say, Mr.

Jones, I will bid you farewell. I look forward to dealing with the next mayor about the excavation."

"That'll be twenty years from now," Mayor Jones managed to choke out, and the stranger laughed at him. I was very glad that he wasn't laughing at me.

"Mademoiselle, will you do me the honor of accompanying me?" The stranger finished his words with a polite bow to me.

"My pleasure, sir." I'd heard a girl say that in the movies and it seemed fitting for this gentleman. Then he smiled at me and offered me his arm. Suddenly the two nasty men and their mumbled curses fell away into nothingness. I was going for a drive with a fine man.

He seated me in the car with a flourish, waiting to be sure that I was comfortable and my dress tucked neatly inside. I wondered if he'd reach for me after we drove off but decided being groped would be a small payment for rescuing me from Bixby.

"Allow me to introduce myself, mademoiselle. My name is," he finished with something French and complicated. I blinked, caught off-guard by a formal introduction.

"Mr. Jim, Jimmy?" I tried, stumbling over the occasion and the foreign name.

He grinned at that. "Yes, please call me Jimmy. It will do very well."

"Anne Smith," I mumbled, flushing red over my clumsiness. I hadn't thought that I could blush about anything after working at Miss Jessie's.

"Where should I take you, Miss Smith?"

"Miss Jessie's house. It's right next to the bridge." I was surprised at his ignorance. We drove in silence for the few minutes it took to cross the bridge and park in front of Miss Jessie's.

That rundown collection of buildings had never looked more wretched than with that lovely car in front. The shabbiest building was the main house, with the rabbit's warren of boarders' rooms trailing behind it. A row of trees shaded the yard and shielded any cars parked there from notice. The trees also sheltered the household's chickens, as was common back then.

Scamp, a big yellow mutt and the leader of Miss Jessie's watchdogs, came rushing over to greet the car. I petted him and gave him the last scraps of my chicken sandwich.

Jimmy spoke quietly to Scamp and the other dogs when they investigated him. He squatted down on his heels and held out his hand, which Scamp sniffed warily before wagging his tail. Scamp's enthusiasm built when Jimmy gave him an expert ear rub.

"Thank you for the ride, Jimmy. You don't have to see me in."

"Are you sure you'll be all right? Mr. Jones and his man aren't the best men for a lady to spend time with."

I nearly laughed at that. If the mayor and Bixby came by later in the evening, I'd spend time doing anything they wanted. Just like any other girl there would. They were the only exceptions to Miss Jessie's rules, and I know she hated them for that.

"I'll be fine."

Jimmy studied me then and I think he saw everything I wasn't saying about those two. He gave me my suitcase only after he looked back down the road to town.

"I'll be by later to see how you're doing." He touched his hat to me and waited to see me go in.

I spent the rest of the evening wondering if Jimmy would come by. All types of men came to Miss Jessie's but I'd never seen him there. I didn't think he'd need to pay a woman for the act but you could say that about many of Miss Jessie's regulars. Still, Jimmy was a handsome man and he'd treated me very well. I kept imagining what he'd be like to spend fifteen minutes with.

The evening was a strange one. It saw very few clients, some spectacular lightning, but no rain. We boarders spent our time waiting in the small sitting room, staring at the bell on the wall, which announced a client's arrival, and jumping whenever a particularly loud thunderbolt hit.

By one o'clock, I was counting the minutes until three when Miss Jessie would close the door to new clients. Linda and Clare, two of the other boarders, were giggling and laughing in a corner. They were quieter about their love games in the sitting room than they were in their shared bedroom. I envied them their fun, while I wished I didn't have the room next to them.

Jimmy came at two o'clock when I'd given up on seeing him. We filed into the main room and seated ourselves demurely on the straight-back chairs lined up in a row. Another row of chairs faced ours for the clients to sit on, which made it easy for Miss Jessie to manage matters from her post at one end.

But Jimmy stood by the door next to Miss Jessie, calm and proud. He looked like a gentleman waiting for his guests to be seated, rather than the typical nervous client. Miss Jessie wasn't quite frowning, which meant that she didn't like his behavior but she couldn't manage to change it.

A rustle ran through the boarders as they saw him. I was prepared for his good looks and fine clothes but they'd never seen the like before. Linda and Clare sat up straighter, openly preening, while some of the others twitched their clothes and struck poses. They only used the attitudes permitted under Miss Jessie's rules but they still tried to catch his attention.

Jimmy ignored them until Miss Jessie nodded at him. Then he strolled directly to me and held out his hand. I put mine into it and he lifted me to my feet, as easily as any Victorian gentleman at a dance. He tucked my hand into the crook of his arm and sauntered toward the door, which led to the boarders' rooms. The other boarders murmured but didn't say anything out loud. I was as surprised as they were by his behavior.

I led him down the long hallway until we reached my room, careful to slow down at every change of ceiling height or flooring. The hallway was at least straight but it showed all the signs of having been built as casually as the rooms it opened to.

"Would you care to sit down?" I invited, as soon as I closed the door behind us. I was pink with embarrassment at seeing him here but I wanted to touch him. I wanted to do things with him that I'd heard whispers of but never tried. I was sure that he knew activities that would scandalize Miss Jessie.

"If you will join me, Miss Smith."

I nodded and perched on the edge of the bed. I was glad that he obviously hadn't paid with a chicken, as most clients did. Those birds were messy and noisy, which would have ruined his elegant suit.

"Uh, the longest you can stay here is fifteen minutes," I started with the last part of the standard speech.

And stopped on that note when his eyebrows went up. It was the first time I'd seen him surprised.

"Fifteen minutes, my dear? Forgive me for asking this, but is fifteen minutes usually long enough for your satisfaction?"

I stared at him. When had my satisfaction started to matter?

Jimmy smiled at me, a very masculine look of knowledge and anticipation.

"We will share an hour together, Anne. Then you can tell me how much time you prefer a gentleman to spend on your pleasure."

I blinked, considering how long it had taken the few previous times when I'd really enjoyed matters. His arm slid around me and I leaned against him, quite happy that he'd moved to the bed and was taking charge. I did feel obliged to ask a question.

"But Miss Jessie's rules say . . ." My voice trailed off when he kissed my hair, then lifted a strand and smelled it. I stared at him in the mirror, shocked and delighted at the gentleness. My senses started to consider him even more intriguing than my mind's estimation of his manners.

"Relax, sweet Anne. I will deal with Miss Jessie."

I nodded a little, afraid to break the connection with his hand. He played with my hair, seeming to enjoy my curls and the weight against his hand. I closed my eyes when he kissed my hand. He trailed kisses over every inch, then turned it over and nipped the mound at the base of my thumb. I gasped and jumped as a surge shot straight from his teeth into my body's center. I moaned when he licked the drop of blood and kissed away the small hurt.

Jimmy spent a very long time on my hands before his mouth found my wrists. I stroked his head as he nuzzled and nipped each pulse point into life. I unbuttoned my dress and slid a sleeve down my shoulder, wordlessly encouraging him to continue farther up that arm.

I think Miss Jessie knocked on the door while my dress was down to my waist. I'm not sure though because I wasn't thinking very clearly by then. I didn't hear her knock again but I think the Angel Gabriel could have sounded his horn without my hearing.

I do know that the feel of his hands and mouth on my breasts excited me like nothing I had ever felt before. He didn't grab at them the way so many men did. Instead he traced every vein from my shoulders and ribs out till it ended. He stayed away from my aureoles until I was frankly begging him to continue. Then he suckled me in long steady pulls, bringing as much of my breast as he could into his mouth's hot, wet warmth. He encouraged the other breast with those long fingers until I was talking language that I'd never thought to say.

His hand found me deep below. I twisted against it and tried to encourage it. I needed more of it than the single finger that traced my folds.

"Show me what you want, my dear." I shook my head, unable to imagine how to tell a man what I'd never discussed before. But he asked me again, that lovely voice of his flowing into my ears and through my body.

Finally I grabbed his hand and placed it on my bud, begging him to get to work. He rewarded me by attending exactly the spot that craved him, varying the pressure and stroke until I cursed and clutched at him. The climax found parts of me that had never joined in pleasure before.

I opened my eyes to find him leaning over me, smiling.

"Why?" I managed to croak.

Jimmy shrugged. "I enjoyed watching you hit your peak. And now, we shall explore conversations with other parts of your body."

My jaw dropped. If he could manage that with just a few fingers, what else could he do? I turned my head away, trying to recover myself somewhat and saw the bedside clock. Twenty minutes had passed. "What about Miss Jessie? You should be leaving."

"Do you want me to?"

"No! But she always insists." I stopped when his finger touched my mouth. I scarcely breathed while he traced the outline of my lips. My tongue crept out, found the callused tip, and delicately explored it. I'd never known what a man's hand tasted like.

"She came." Jimmy leaned closer to me and I closed my eyes. "She left at my request and promised not to return." He kissed me when I opened my mouth to ask him why she'd done that. But I forgot my questions under his sweet seduction.

Some say there are a thousand ways to kiss, and I swear that Jimmy knew all of them. Knew and taught me some of them that night. The best were deep kisses that traveled through me like a drug, until my entire body was on fire for him. I twisted restlessly under him, fondling his head and neck and shoulders. Caressing anything and everything I could reach, anxious to touch as much of him as I could, while he showed me what it felt like to be an attractive woman.

He rid me of my clothes at some point. I've no idea when because it didn't matter to me. I did understand that if I asked him to do anything, whether in words or deeds, he would do it until I was most pleased. He made me tell him what I wanted and rewarded me for every request.

Jimmy attended to the obvious parts of me, especially my breasts and between my legs. But he also enjoyed other places, like my navel, which seemed to have a direct link to my core. When he rolled me on my stomach, I writhed and sobbed and pounded my fists while he learned every sensitive spot on my back. And when he buried his face to drink my dew while his finger dipped into my backside, I screamed so loudly that I didn't hear the thunder after lightning brightened the room.

I recovered myself slowly and watched the lightning. It was worse than it had been before midnight and I was silent for a few minutes. Scamp and the other dogs were barking, in warning but not alarm. Linda and Clare were playing next door, producing long sighs that echoed through the house. I knew they weren't too serious since Clare wasn't laughing continuously. But I missed Jimmy's warmth, even with the sheet drawn up to my neck, and turned to find him.

He was standing at the door, frowning as he listened. I stood up and grabbed my robe before joining him. I could hear Miss Jessie arguing with a man. I pressed closer and knew whom she was talking to.

Mayor Jones was back. I heard the back screen door slam as another lightning bolt shot through the sky. I leaned back against the wall and closed my eyes, sending up a prayer.

"Anne, dear."

I looked up at Jimmy. His face was set and hard. If he hadn't just taught me how tender a man could be with a woman, I would have run from the look on his face.

He kissed my forehead in reassurance and I relaxed.

"Wait here while I deal with him. Don't leave the room, no matter what happens."

"But," I began, trying to say that he should leave before Bixby found him. Jimmy chuckled softly at the look on my face.

"He can't hurt me, dear. Promise me that you won't leave the room."

I hesitated for a moment, then yielded and agreed.

Jimmy left the room without another word. I pressed my ear against the door, trying to hear what was going on. I heard Miss Jessie yell, a harsh sound that stopped abruptly.

I couldn't bear not knowing what was happening. So I opened the door and looked out, being careful to keep my body inside the room.

Mayor Jones was charging through the kitchen door, with Bixby at his shoulder. His face was near purple with anger but he was silent, a sure sign of terrible fury. I couldn't see Miss Jessie and I feared for her life.

Jimmy stood in front of my door, with a knife in each hand. The single lightbulb in the ceiling turned their polished steel into cold flames. Then the knives took flight.

Mayor Jones stopped cold, a knife in the doorframe on either side of his head. His eyes darted from one side to the other. He glared at Jimmy and a big Colt revolver appeared in his hand.

Jimmy laughed. My blood ran cold at the sound. He lifted his hands and flexed his fingers like a pianist. The knives quivered in the wood and then took flight again. He laughed yet again when the knives blossomed in his hands, glowing like hellfire.

Another lightning bolt struck very close to us. Its thunder followed immediately and shook the house. I could smell the burning ozone through the open windows. Lightning cracked again and again. Linda and Clare were chuckling, their cries punctuated by more lightning.

"Damn you, you fancy lawyer!" Mayor Jones hissed. "Bixby, get him."

Bixby stopped. Another lightning bolt showed his wide eyes as he stared over Mayor Jones's shoulder at Jimmy. Jimmy smiled at him, turning the knives in his fingers.

"Yes, please do, Bixby. It would give me the greatest pleasure to send you straight to hell."

"Damn you, Bixby, don't listen to him. He's just a

pretty boy. You've killed bigger men than him before. Get him!" the mayor shouted and stepped aside so Bixby could pass.

Bixby took a step forward. Jimmy balanced a knife, making a show of preparing to throw it. Bixby hesitated, watching Jimmy as if he'd never seen his like before. He took another step, hesitantly this time. Thunder rolled outside like a battalion on the march. Then a knife bloomed in Bixby's hat and pinned it to the wall.

Bixby opened his mouth in a scream but made no sound as he stared at Jimmy. Jimmy snapped his fingers and the knife left the hat to return to him.

Bixby backed up slowly and bumped against Mayor Jones. He looked at the mayor as if they were strangers and then shoved him aside.

"Bixby, where are you going? You can kill him."

"No, no I can't. Not tonight, not ever." Another step took Bixby back inside the kitchen.

"Bixby."

Bixby froze under the lash of Jimmy's voice. "Yes, sir?" he quavered.

"The next night you sleep in Texas or Oklahoma will be your last. Understand?"

"Yes, sir. I'll remember that, sir. I'm leaving now, sir, for good. Sir."

"Bixby!" the mayor shouted and was answered by the screen door's slam. A car started and left within a minute.

"Jones."

Mayor Jones turned around slowly and looked at Jimmy. He displayed more courage than I would have. Or was it stupidity?

"You're going to resign as mayor and you're never coming back to this house. Do you understand?"

"Like hell I'll do that, boy. You may have some pretty knife tricks but they're no match for a good Colt." Mayor Jones shook himself slightly and pointed the revolver at Jimmy.

"You blind fool." The knives slid back up Jimmy's sleeves.

A trio of lightning bolts burst overhead, so close together as to be almost one. The ceiling lights hissed and sparked then winked out, as if acknowledging a greater power. Mayor Jones cursed. I glimpsed a white blur flying down the hall.

Another burst of green-tinted light showed a hawk beating at the mayor's face with its wings and talons. The mayor screamed and tried to fight it. He dropped the gun, which went off. He howled then and ran for the kitchen door, limping badly. The hawk chased him, still attacking.

I ran to the window and looked out over the yard. The mayor soon bolted out the back door and paused, desperately looking for an escape. Miss Jessie's car was locked up in the garage as always and the yard was empty of clients' cars. The hawk swooped down on him and the mayor cursed.

Scamp barked, the clear command of a general summoning his troops. He had always hated the mayor and was kept locked up when the mayor called. Suddenly all the dogs were there, barking and growling as they snapped at the mayor's legs.

Lightning flashed again and again as Jones ran for the trees that stood between the yard and the highway. He clambered up with surprising agility for a man of his age and weight, hindered further by a bleeding leg. But all the commotion and his clumsiness disturbed the roosting chickens. They too descended on him, sending him farther up into the tree until he was so well wedged in between branches that they couldn't reach him.

Thunder rolled. The skies opened and poured down rain. I hastily ducked back inside my room but kept trying to see where Jimmy was. Every other boarder had poked her head outside and was staring at the mayor.

"Best get back inside, young lady," Miss Jessie said from just outside my window. She had a towel pressed to her head but looked otherwise none the worse for wear.

"But—" I started to protest.

"Your caller will be returning to you in a moment. You'd best be prepared to thank him for all he's done on your behalf."

"Oh yes, ma'am!" I started to shut the window.

"Anne, remember my rules. Callers can stay with a young lady only until eleven in the morning."

"Thank you, ma'am!" Jimmy had become a caller, not a client. Now I had hours to spend learning from him.

I leaned farther out the window, trying to find Jimmy so I could tell him. Slams marked windows being shut as the boarders settled themselves again, like horses entering the stable at night. The hens clucked in a rather irritated fashion as they rediscovered comfortable places to sleep. Scamp and his cohorts barked at the incensed mayor, flinging themselves up the tree in a victory celebration.

Suddenly, a man's hands slipped around me and cupped my breasts inside my robe. My nipples quickly welcomed the familiar touch, hardening as they surged forward eagerly. He rubbed his hips against me. I could feel his hard ridge rub my robe's silk up and down the crack in my backside.

I swear my body melted at the touch. I wriggled against Jimmy and tried to turn. He squeezed me fiercely and I yelped. I stood stock-still and felt my body liquefy in yearning.

"Did you obey me, sweet Anne?" His voice was low and rough, a hunter's growl in my ear.

"Y-yes," I stammered. Even my mind was yielding to his body. I still remember the scent of his fine cologne as my hips quivered helplessly against him.

"Then lift your robe and bend over."

I groaned at his command. My hands fumbled as I obeyed him. I didn't want to wait even the few seconds that it took to bare myself for him. Then I braced myself on the window ledge, as eager and willing as any mare in heat, totally heedless of the rain pounding my hair.

He came into me on a hard surge that slammed me forward. My hips were trapped between his legs and the windowsill. My shoulders went down but my head came up as I arched. I moaned as my insides adapted to him, welcoming his cock into my wet, needy depths. I had never felt so much before. I hadn't known just how good it could be to have a man fill you, showing what a woman's flesh and blood was made for.

Jimmy moved slowly at first until I learned how to move with him. His hand found my bud and played it, until I moaned louder than Linda and Clare put together. Water pulsed over my head and shoulders as I rocked in and out of the window under him. Then he thrust harder and faster, altering his angle until he was pounding a single spot deep inside. I came with a rush the first time he hit that point. But he did it again and again until every inch of me burst into fireworks.

When I could think again, I was lying on the bed, my robe hung over the chair, looking as limp as I felt. My hair was wrapped in a towel and my shoulders were only slightly damp. The window was closed, a slight barrier against the world beyond. Jimmy was taking his clothes off, contemplating me.

I reached up and took off the towel, the only thing that hid me from him. I stretched for him and displayed myself shamelessly. I wanted more of his magnificent body. I wanted to learn and experience and enjoy my womanhood. His eyes glowed when I ran a finger between my legs. I liked that reaction so I did it again, letting him see just how good he made me feel.

"Show me more."

I blinked, uncertain what he was talking about. He could see every inch. Then I realized that he wanted to see my emotions, my pleasure, my willingness.

So I touched myself again as I had never done before. I circled and played as my fingers learned how to awaken the excitement that he had taught me.

I watched Jimmy closely while I did so, my eyes caressing the strong masculine form that the fine tailoring had hidden. He had wonderful sweeps of muscle across his chest and a flat stomach that looked fit to lift a horse.

I sighed when I saw his legs, with their long corded muscles flowing down to catch his knees then swelling briefly to hold his calves' speed and determination. Finally ending at neat, square ankles so unlike a woman's in their ability to carry his strength forward. His broad shoulders were perfectly suited to his height and carried his strong neck and head well. As for his cock, well, I had seen many before but his was especially handsome, since I knew so well what a wonderful lover he was.

Jimmy's slender fingers toyed with his cock, sliding the loose skin up and down all of the hard shaft. I gasped when he pulled that skin over the fat tip, deliberately inciting more wet beads to emerge from the narrow slit. His eyelids drooped sensually, their thick lashes almost concealing his blue eyes.

He smiled and I saw a glint of white teeth against his lip. I blinked and he curled his lip back. He deliberately showed me his fangs. I choked as I wondered what he really wanted from me. I could pretend that the hawk had no connection to him but this was different.

My finger hesitated and my bud pulsed restlessly. My body's heat increased under his dark blue gaze.

I remembered how many times he could have injured me as Bixby had. How many times he had given delight to me. How he always protected me from any harm.

My finger moved again and I spread my legs wider in invitation.

"You're going to be very sore," Jimmy growled.

I laughed and held out my arms to him. He came onto me in a rush that wiped away every other memory of a man in my bed. I wrapped my arms and legs around him and pulled him against me until his heat burned into me. His fat cock rubbed my folds and I pushed against it. I arched my neck and caressed his head as his mouth tasted my shoulder. But I wanted everything he could show me.

"More, please," I begged, stroking his hair and wriggling against him.

He came into me hard and fast, slamming into action. I dug my heels into his back and thrust myself onto him. We rode each other like wild cavalry that night, galloping headlong into a passion that asked only for honesty and willingness. I sobbed his name when ecstasy flared hot and bright, as I felt his fangs sink into my blood.

I don't know how often he had me. I don't clearly remember how many positions that we found, just that I always liked each one. Some were excellent, like his chest hair rubbing my back while my backside snuggled his stomach and his cock nudged that hidden spot inside me. Some were sweetly enjoyable, like sitting on his lap while his arms leisurely lifted me up and down his hard cock. But I could always smell him on my skin as his cream overflowed my core and glided over my thighs.

Finally, I fell asleep with my face buried in the pillow.

I blinked sleepily when he woke me, and reached for the covers, trying to go back to sleep.

"Sweet Anne, you look like a little hen, who's finally found a comfortable roost." He dropped a kiss on my hair. "Rest then and be happy when you face the world again."

He kissed me on the cheek and I mumbled something. I was asleep before the door opened.

I awoke to the sound of laughter ringing through the room. At some point during the night, after the rain had finally stopped, Jimmy had opened the window to let the cool air in. I stretched, discovering twinges in places that had never known them before. I purred, remembering how I had gained those aches.

I listened without opening my eyes. Linda and Clare were laughing but so were many other people. I got up and went over to the window, making sure to fasten my robe snugly first. There were a few drops of blood on my neck but nothing that mattered.

A dozen or more people were standing in the road, looking up at the tree and pointing at Jones. He was a wretched sight, with scratches on his face and hands from the birds and a bloody trouser leg. His clothes and hair were smeared with chicken deposits. Now he was trying to find a way down from the treetop but couldn't find a branch that looked sturdy enough for his weight. At least his wounded leg didn't seem to be giving him any more trouble than its mate.

While I stood there, another car stopped to see what all the commotion was about. Its passengers soon joined the others in poking fun at Jones. By the time I finished dressing, every resident of Susanville had found an excuse to see the mayor in that tree. The fire department's truck suffered one of its frequent breakdowns so Jones didn't touch ground until afternoon.

Miss Jessie spoke to all of her boarders over breakfast that morning. She informed us that she was sure that all of her young ladies had seen nothing unusual on Saturday night or Sunday morning. We nodded dutifully, our mouths full of the excellent food. None of us would dare speak about the mayor's misadventures anywhere that Miss Jessie might hear.

Then she told us that she was taking a vacation for the next month and closing the house. She frowned at the girls who objected to that and reminded them just whose business this was. When they were silent and trying to hide their worries, she announced that every boarder would receive one hundred dollars in cash, to help overcome any discomfort that the closing would cause.

This sum silenced even the noisiest boarder. One hundred dollars was a fortune then to girls like us.

She finished by saying that she hoped we would all remember her kindness and return when she reopened. Most of them did.

I heard that when Jones showed up at the courthouse on Monday morning, no one could look at him without laughing. He was in a foul temper, of course, but the ridicule was worse to him than anything else. He went home within an hour and was never seen again in Susanville. Gossip had it that he and his wife moved to Florida, where they lost a fortune playing at real estate.

Linda and Clare became backup singers for a gospel music star, who took them to Nashville. They wrote songs for him, including one about the Susanville chicken roost. He recorded it for a country music album and it was played for a time on the radio. But mostly he stayed with gospel and the song faded. Except, of course, in my house since I have a copy of every song Linda and Clare ever wrote or recorded.

You've heard the story from there a thousand times. How I took Scamp with me to San Antonio to visit you and Aunt Mabel. How I went to the dance and met Ezra, the handsomest man I've ever seen in a uniform.

How we married within the month and he's been your father and my husband ever since. How your brother Michael arrived within a year, James three years later, and . . .

Never mind; you've heard it before or remember it for yourself.

I told him the truth about my history, of course, before we married. All of it, including the lessons Jimmy taught me that night, but no mention of any individual men. Mercifully, Ezra has never been jealous of my past, choosing to live in the present and future like the career soldier he was. He often teases me about being a curious wench who never tires of exploring her man.

Sometimes, though, I pray for Jimmy, who deserves better than the loneliness I saw on that Susanville street. I hope one day he lays down his ancient grief and finds happiness in a woman's arms.

the storm cellar

a tale of don rafael perez

It was a fine summer day in the Texas Hill Country, meaning that it was hot and steamy. The weather promised a storm, hopefully only a thunderstorm and nothing worse.

Elizabeth Smith sat peacefully at the kitchen table, her gnarled hands shelling peas with the careless ease learned from decades of practice. The scene was the same as it had been when she left to marry her second husband almost seventy years ago. The barn was just visible beyond her small garden, blocking the view of her son John's house with all its modern conveniences. She preferred to stay in the house her father had built, where she could avoid any squeaky floorboard. Not, of course, that her grandson Henry permitted squeaks in any building that his family lived in.

Henry liked to manage both people and things, which was probably why his daughter Mary was over here now, far from the swimming pool or the air-conditioned house. She paced around the kitchen, unable to settle, her eyes red-rimmed and dull from too little sleep and too many tears.

Elizabeth sighed, recognizing her own past in the younger woman's actions.

"Would you like some coffee, Gran?"

"Thank you, Mary, thank you. A cup of coffee would be very nice. Do you know where everything is? Of course, you do; you've visited me here a thousand times." Elizabeth settled back and let Mary pour the coffee. But she kept a thread of talk spinning between them.

"I remember when I saw you in the hospital the day you were born. And when you and Joe got married here at the old family ranch. You two looked so fine that day."

Elizabeth clucked at her clumsiness when the tears spilled silently down Mary's face. She got up with a spryness belying her age and wrapped her arms around her great-granddaughter. Mary buried her face against the familiar shoulder and shook with her sobs.

"There, there now, honey. You can cry if you want to. Joe may still be alive. They just said he was missing over there in Southeast Asia; they didn't know if he was dead for sure. There's still hope. There, there . . ."

Elizabeth patted Mary's shoulder and kept talking to her, her words a soft croon against the quiet afternoon.

"Sometimes it's best to just cry it out. A good bit of crying can be just the thing for a person, like a thunderstorm bringing rain and washing the earth clean. But some storms aren't like that at all. They take life away. I can still remember feeling my baby ripped out of my arms by the big hurricane." She stopped, reliving that agony again. It always hurt; she'd just learned ways to live with the pain. She went on, trying to explain those lessons in words.

"When that happens, you've just got to follow the good earth's example: Hunker down and try to survive until it's time to sprout again."

She fell silent and simply held Mary as the tears gradually ended.

"But, Gran, didn't you pray that your husband lived through that storm?" Mary stood up a little shakily and accepted Elizabeth's handkerchief to blow her nose with.

"Honey, I didn't see my husband swept away by the water but I heard him scream when it took him. A week later, I identified his body after the tide brought it back to the land. So I hoped and prayed during that week. But when I saw what was left of him, well, I was more than ready to let him go to the darkness of the grave."

Mary shuddered. Her former restlessness returned and she checked the clock. The peach pies wouldn't be done for another half hour and the kitchen was becoming very hot.

"Would you like to sit on the porch, Gran? Maybe you could tell me a story, like you used to when I was small," Mary asked wistfully.

"Of course, I'd be glad to, honey." Elizabeth smiled at her, remembering the bright-faced child with her long pigtails who was as ready to hear a tall tale as she was to play pranks on her older brothers. It was a terrible thing to see so much fear and pain on a girl who hadn't yet seen her twentieth birthday. But Mary was older now than Elizabeth had been when she lost both husband and baby to the great Galveston hurricane.

"Would you like to hear a story about a tornado? Perhaps you're ready to hear about storms and how folks find shelter from them."

Mary agreed eagerly, clearly hoping for one of Gran's tales to distract her, as they always had before. Elizabeth smiled to herself. She waited until they were both settled in rockers on the porch before beginning.

✦

I was twenty-five when this tornado hit. You've seen the picture of me from that age: five feet of hardworking Texas woman. My curves were all in the right places, if I do say so myself, and I had lots of yellow curls. Men paid a lot of calls but I didn't pay them any heed. I was living back here at home after my husband and baby were swept away by that big hurricane at Galveston. Hundreds of miles of land felt like a safe distance between me and the sea. I wasn't much interested in living, let alone getting close to a man.

It was Monday and I was doing the wash and the baking. Ma and Pa had gone flying out of the house at first light when my brother-in-law came by. My sister Betty thought the time had finally come to deliver her first. The three of them were buzzing with excitement that I just couldn't share. So I stayed home to do the chores.

You grew up with electricity. Do you remember hearing just how much work washday took? All day feeding that stove to get hot water for the wash, then using the hot oven to bake bread and sweets for the rest of the week. It was just what I needed though: hard labor that left me no room for thinking about anything else.

I did notice the weather though. It was hot, humid, and still. Skies were clear, at least in the morning. The light turned a bit green in the afternoon but I thought that was just the angle of the sun.

It wasn't until I went out to take down the dry clothes that I really thought about a storm. The wind slammed the screen door behind me and I looked up at the sky, trying to see the full moon rising. Big black clouds were boiling up, racing overhead like armies in a battlefield. It seemed like they could fall on top of me at any minute, crushing me into the ground. The wind pushed me back against the house. The sky was dark, growing blacker every minute.

That was when I heard the noise for the first time. It seemed like every bit of air clamored and rumbled. I'd never heard that sound before but I knew what it meant. There was a twister close by—real close by. I might not have time to get to the storm cellar. . . .

Thank you, Mary. Coffee is good for putting heart into a person, even when she's just reliving old scares. Now, where was I?

The wind howled louder and suddenly I could move. I had to reach the storm cellar on the other side of the barn before the tornado caught me. Normally I was afraid of that dark hole and the bugs inside but not now. There was no time to be scared of anything except this storm.

I picked up my skirts and ran as fast as I could. The demons of hell grabbed at my heels as I went. All my hairpins were lost before I passed the barn. But I reached the top of the bank and slid down the other side on my fanny to the storm cellar. Then I grabbed the trap doors and tried to pull them open. But the winds kept whipping the doors shut.

Suddenly a man's arm came over mine on the handle. Together we pulled it open. He pushed me in and I fell down the steps. I shouted at him to get in. Moments later, he was on the steps, fighting the tornado for the doors.

I caught one glimpse of him in the little bit of light. He looked Spaniard but he was a big man, taller even than Betty's husband. He had a harsh profile, with a hook nose. Black hair, black eyes against that olive skin. He was dressed in a black suit, too; fine gentlemen's clothing. Then he shouted something and yanked and the doors fell into place, closing out the strange skies and the storm beyond.

The tornado still raged outside, trying to break into our hiding place. I screamed when something banged into the doors. I couldn't hear myself think over the noise. Then he was on his knees beside me.

I went into his arms like a homing pigeon. I hid my face against his shoulder and cried, trembling like a cobweb. He tried to calm me, saying that we were safe and the tornado wouldn't hurt the ranch. He told me not to think about the storm but I kept on crying. Finally the flood of tears was gone and I calmed down.

It was dark down there and the wind was quieter, although I could still hear things crashing in it. He released me carefully and I took a deep breath. He moved away and I heard a match strike.

Soft golden lantern light lit the cellar. It both softened and emphasized his face's harshness and reminded me of how the green light had outlined the washing that had been hung out to dry before the storm.

I stared at him, seeing an attractive man but not one that my family would ever approve of. He watched me with equal intensity and I began to feel enticing, as long-dormant emotions began to stir. His eyes were a mite reserved though, like clouds in a blue sky that hint of a storm but cause no problems for the moment. A coil of heat flickered in my belly. The cellar doors rattled but I paid little heed.

I blinked at my own thoughts. Then I looked at him again, openly studying his magnificent body under the fine clothing. My stomach clenched again and I felt a little damp between my legs.

His nostrils flared and heat burned in his eyes under my stare. He looked at me as if I were the most desirable woman he had ever seen. I ran my tongue over my lips, moistening them. His dark gaze followed the movement and I became wetter.

He walked toward me slowly, the beams brushing his hair. He glided like a cougar, arrogant in his own masculinity and confident of his welcome. I trembled before his strut but lifted my chin proudly, my eyes locked to his.

I put out a hand to him and he took it. He lifted it slowly to his mouth. He kissed each finger and then the back of my hand. Then his fingers shifted and his mouth tasted my palm. I could feel his lips caressing me before his tongue moved to the pulse in my wrist. My hand stroked his strong jaw and I moaned. He smiled slightly and repeated the caress on my other hand. The wind outside howled louder and my blood raced faster.

He fondled my cheek with his other hand and I rubbed against it, treasuring the touch. My nipples hardened like rosebuds as I shivered. His hand slipped under my chin and lifted my head. I felt like a moonflower seed, buried in the earth but waiting for the first touch of rain to start sprouting.

Then his mouth touched mine. I opened my mouth and his tongue took advantage of the opportunity. He tasted sweet, like fresh water from a deep well. Our mouths explored each other slowly, gradually moving closer and closer, until finally our tongues were entwined like sweet pea vines.

His hands slipped over my shoulders and down my arms, smoothing away my clothes. I trembled and leaned into his touch, enjoying the damp air on my skin. Then he leaned back and looked at me. I stood proud and tall under his hot gaze, like a sunflower reaching for the sky. He smiled at me and traced my nipple. He murmured something about honey before his lips took possession of my breast. A jolt of fire ran through my body and I arched back against his arm.

Somewhere the wind was shrieking beyond the cellar. I was hot and wet at the same time, shuddering as life flowed through my body in response to him. . . .

Sorry, honey. I guess I must have lost track of my story for a moment.

That man's touch sent devils dancing through my body like the tornado whipping the earth beyond the doors. I burst into life like the first green plants in spring. He brought sounds out of me to match the wind's voice—low moans, solid groans, even shrieks of astonishment. I could feel my blood surging through my veins, like sap rising through a tree in the spring. The man built my excitement and yet I felt safe. I could laugh at the storm pounding outside while the dance of life raged behind the cellar doors, sheltering us from the tempest.

He fed my pleasure for a long time, there in the dark. His hands were magical, coaxing and urging me onward, while his voice crooned of the delights offered by my body. He said I was fairer than lilies, sweeter than roses, softer than camellias. I tumbled time and time again into rapture.

I could sense his excitement as his voice became uneven and his hands harsher. I could barely hear him over the wind's noise, thundering like a freight train above us. But I was braver now, anxious to taste a stronger possession, like a summer thunderstorm after the gentle rains of spring. I begged him to give us both completion.

Finally his mouth moved over my neck and he drank my blood, as the life he'd given me flowed back into him. My cries of rapture were drowned by the tornado above us, as it burst from earth to sky. . . .

⚜

The two women sat silently on the porch together, watching the rain fall softly from the afternoon storm.

"Would you like some more coffee, Gran?" Mary asked, finally breaking the quiet.

"Thank you, Mary. A little warm-up for my coffee would be nice." Elizabeth studied Mary's face before asking her question. "Did I scandalize you, honey? The story is a mite racy."

Mary smiled, her face settling awkwardly but willingly into the almost forgotten expression. "Oh no, Gran, you didn't upset me. I think I feel more jealous than embarrassed." She gave Elizabeth a quick hug and the two women clung to each other briefly.

"And I do enjoy your stories, whether or not they're perfectly true," Mary whispered against Elizabeth's hair before going inside, whistling a radio tune.

Elizabeth heard the timer ring, followed by the smell of fresh peach pies set out to cool. Mary returned with fresh coffee for both of them, which the women settled back into the rockers to enjoy.

"What happened after that, Gran?"

"Ma and Pa found me the next morning, asleep in the storm cellar. We laughed and cried together, the tears flowing freely in the joy of reunion. We didn't say much though, especially not with so much work to be done helping the neighbors rebuild. The tornado had turned away from our place at the last minute, just before our storm cellar. The two red marks on my neck were gone within a couple days."

Elizabeth touched the place where the marks had

once shown, her eyes absent. She didn't notice Mary's eyes widen at the confirming gesture. Elizabeth shook herself briefly to come back to the present and went on.

"I met your great-grandfather at church the following Sunday. You know that part of the story, how he'd come down to help his cousin rebuild, how I walked out with him as soon as he asked. I knew what I wanted as soon as I saw him. I knew he brought the deep springs of life to set roots in."

The phone's peremptory squall broke their peace. Mary bolted upright and then froze. She stared at Elizabeth, frozen by equal parts of hope and doubt. Elizabeth released her to act.

"Would you answer that for me, honey? It might be a call for you. . . ."

Mary ran inside, slamming the door against the wall in her haste. Elizabeth listened unabashedly to the one-sided conversation, which quickly brought her hands up in gladness.

"Joe's alive! Thanks be to the Almighty, he's coming back to Mary," Elizabeth praised, and bent her head to give thanks.

Mary came out of the house a few minutes after she'd hung up. Her face was streaming with tears, shining like the roses in the garden under the storm.

"Did you hear, Gran? Joe's coming home," Mary

whispered, her voice breaking on the words. She gulped and dropped to her knees in front of Elizabeth.

Elizabeth stroked the shining hair lovingly.

"That's all right, Mary; you just go ahead and cry. Sometimes it's good to remember how life can come back from where it's hiding in the dark."

peppermint candy

a tale of jean-marie st. just

It feels so good to be back at your house, Joan! I know these banquets are important but high heels always kill my feet. Thanks for the wine; I really appreciate your taking the time to find me some pink wine.

You're right: I don't know who shot J. R. Ewing, and I don't care. Even if that does make me the most out-of-touch person in America! My daughters watch that show every week, which gives me time to read cases.

Yup, I do like being a judge and I do like reading the law. . . . And I don't like giving speeches any more than

I ever did, although it's easier when it's for a gaggle of female law students.

Yes, I'm stalling! But I'll tell you the real story of how I fell in love with the law.

It was back when I first came to Austin from West Texas. I'd grown up in a one-horse town where everyone was either a rancher or the wife, daughter, mother—whatever of a rancher. I was absolutely determined that I wasn't going to spend the rest of my life on a ranch. After some effort, I managed to persuade my pa to let me go to college if I paid for it. You've met him; you can imagine how much persuasion that took!

Anyway, I got a scholarship and made it to the University three days after my eighteenth birthday. The scholarship didn't cover everything so I found myself a very cheap boardinghouse within sight of the Tower. I saved even more money by doing housework for my landlady. There was a lot of work she wanted done, needed to have done.

Then I started classes and found out very quickly that my little high school in West Texas might have produced good football players but hadn't begun to provide me enough education to keep up with the rest of my class. I began to spend every spare moment at the library, studying like I never had before. Between study-

ing and working for the Landlady from Hell, I barely
had time to eat and sleep.

By the time finals came, I was exhausted and desperate. I had to get an A on the final for American history
just to pass the class and stay in school. I was at the library so often that it's a wonder nobody mistook me for
a bookcase.

I met a really nice guy in the stacks one night when I
was looking for a book on the Constitution. I didn't
think he was anyone my pa would object to: same
height as my brother Harry, tall, brown hair, blue eyes,
fast-moving as a sword, graceful as a girl but powerful
as a cougar. He looked only a few years older than I,
possibly old enough to be a grad student. He had a
French name, Jean-Marie something.

We got to talking about my history class and he was
able to offer me all sorts of tips, which I just tried to
soak up. I was upset when the closing bell rang. I didn't
want to let go of the best talk I'd had on history since ar-
riving at school. He teased me about my disappoint-
ment and offered to help me study the next night, just
before my final.

I wanted to say yes but I knew that my landlady
would never consent to a man visiting me after hours.
She had standards that would put the minister's wife

back home to shame. I tried to explain this to Jean-Marie. He simply smiled at me and told me not to be surprised if I had a visitor the next evening.

The next day was awful. My landlady had a list of chores for me that would amaze Cinderella's stepmother. I didn't even start scrubbing the oven until after doing the supper dishes. So there I was, newspapers spread over the floor and windows wide open to the cold winter air. Even wearing an enormous apron over my faded pink dress and heavy rubber gloves, I still had smudges on my face. My hair was escaping from the bandanna like rats off a sinking ship.

You know, Joan, you really don't have to laugh quite that hard! Why do you think I have a maid now?

So, that's when my landlady came to tell me that a lady had come to call on me. I didn't want to see anyone and told her to say no. But she kept insisting and finally I had to go see the person who'd managed to get the Landlady from Hell to carry a message.

You can imagine my surprise to see the most picture-perfect lady waiting in the front parlor. She was wearing a peppermint pink suit with its full skirt carefully laid out over the sofa. Her outfit was complete, down to matching hat, gloves, purse, and shoes. Then she turned her head and I saw . . . Jean-Marie.

My mouth dropped open. I swear that he made a

prettier girl than I ever have. Even his voice was gorgeous—like Ava Gardner with a French accent. I wanted to scream that it wasn't fair. I wanted to demand how he got his makeup to look that good. And I was suddenly miserably conscious of just how much I looked like Cinderella's poor relation.

I was angry and upset that he was wearing a dress. I started to yell at him but realized quickly that my landlady would be furious. She'd probably throw me out if she knew that a man was visiting me in her house, a man who, even worse, wore women's clothes. I bit my lip, not knowing what to do or say.

Jean-Marie caught my eyes then. He looked tense, which didn't match the self-confident student who'd aided me in the library's stacks. He silently urged me to calm down.

I took a deep breath and sat down. I looked at everything in that overcrowded room except Jean-Marie.

Then I heard my landlady offering to finish in the kitchen so I could visit with Miss Marie for as long as I liked. Jean-Marie accepted that offer promptly, watching the woman serenely now. He reminded me of our barn cats back home: They always presented themselves at the side door at the same time every day for their saucer of food. They never bothered asking for it; they simply expected you to provide it as soon as they appeared. Jean-Marie had the same overwhelming confidence that my landlady would provide what was necessary, just because he wanted it.

I studied Jean-Marie then, trying to see how he did it. How could he look so absolutely confident in a dress? He had been so masculine in the library.

My brother and I had lots of arguments about peppermint candy when we were children. You know, the red-and-white-striped kind? We argued endlessly about whether it was a red candy or a white candy. I started to wonder whether Jean-Marie was masculine or feminine. I started to look for signs of him being a man, under all the stripes of women's clothing.

I could see his shoulders, layered with muscle where a woman's would be fragile bones and smooth skin under the dress. I noticed his wrists, rich with tendons and veins, unlike a woman's delicacy. In fact, his hands reminded me of Errol Flynn from the old movies my mother loves: a swordsman's hands, as quick to caress as to kill. His legs were an athlete's legs, showing corded muscle rather than a woman's sleek lines.

He sat on the boardinghouse sofa like a soldier waiting for a call to arms, ready to move in any direction at a moment's notice. A lady would have alighted on the sofa, relaxing as if in her own home.

I saw more and more of the man as I stared at him:

the strong neck, the hard lines of cheek and jaw, the eyes . . .

I swallowed hard when I looked into his eyes fully. He looked at me as if I were the most beautiful woman in the world. I blushed and looked down at my hands. Then my eyes returned to him.

Jean-Marie stood up with a rustle of petticoats, collected me with a glance, and moved smoothly upstairs. I followed, jealous of how much easier he walked in high-heeled shoes than I ever had. He glided through the house like the big cat he reminded me of. He made going up those steep, narrow stairs look like the simplest thing anyone ever had to do.

I cast a quick glance back downstairs but couldn't see the Landlady from Hell. I took a deep breath and kept going.

My room was upstairs in the attic and looked like a disaster. Books and dirty clothes were scattered around so you could hardly find the furniture. Not that the furniture was much to look at but . . .

Anyway, I gestured helplessly for him to sit down. Jean-Marie sat down on the narrow bed like Grace Kelly and folded his hands. I started to ask questions but he held up one finger. I fell silent and waited too.

Then I heard my landlady huffing up the stairs. It was the first time I'd ever heard her climb them. My jaw dropped when she appeared at my door, carrying coffee and cookies for two. I had no idea she owned a fancy coffeepot. Jean-Marie, of course, accepted the refreshments as a natural part of everyday life and then got the woman out of there. I shut the door after her and looked at Jean-Marie.

He began to chuckle at the look on my face. I started to laugh too. We laughed together until tears ran down my face and I couldn't stand up straight. I collapsed onto the bed against Jean-Marie and hugged him. He kissed the top of my head and held me until I was calmer.

We had coffee after that and talked about history. Jean-Marie had some great stories about the founding fathers, stories that made them real people but that I've never found in a book. He made the Constitution come alive for me as the work of individual men trying to make a better life for their children. I fell in love with those men and their work that night.

Then he started quizzing me. He asked me all of the exam questions, plus a few more that were harder than anything the professor ever thought of. We worked on those questions until I was word perfect. . . .

No more wine please, Joan. What with the banquet, I've had too much already!

When we finished, it was after midnight and could see the full moon through the window. We were sitting on the bed together—well, it was the only place to sit in the room. Jean-Marie had his arm around me. His body was as hot and strong as a sports car on an August day but I could feel his underthings beneath the pink wool. His mascara still looked good even from that close. I could smell his cologne, something spicy and masculine.

I asked him who taught him how to wear pink wool and high heels like that. He smirked and told me that he'd learned from the Sun King. Plus, he'd been an actor and a spy.

I laughed at that. I know the men back then were fancy dressers but still! Then I leaned up and kissed him on the mouth. Well, he'd been so sweet, even if he did stretch the truth, and I had to do something to ruin that lipstick! His feminine disguise was driving me crazy, and I wanted to see more of the man.

Jean-Marie promptly kissed me back. He kissed like an angel, as if he could spend hours and hours making love to my mouth. I figured out real fast that he was a far better kisser than Jerry Black, second-string tackle on my high school's football team and the only fellow I'd ever kissed before.

I enjoyed his kisses and after a while, I started to do

some of the kissing myself. Jean-Marie encouraged me to experiment and, well, time flew by.

Somehow we managed to lie down on the bed, both of our skirts sliding up to our waists. Jean-Marie got my dress open and started fondling my breasts. Pretty soon he had his hand between my legs and I lost all power of rational thought. I felt dizzy and my head was spinning, as if peppermint candy's red and white stripes were swirling around me.

When he moved his mouth back up from my breasts to my mouth, I just grabbed his head and kissed him hard. He gave a satisfied grunt and kissed me as if he couldn't get enough. Mercifully, he was still kissing me when his finger slipped inside me. I screamed when he took me over the edge for the first time in my life but his mouth swallowed the sound.

When I calmed down a bit, he was lying between my legs. He'd put the pillow under my hips and his arms were under my thighs, lifting them up. He'd set aside that pink hat earlier but he still had on the wig with its long brown ringlets flowing over his shoulders. His peppermint-pink skirts rubbed my ankles. But some-how, he didn't look feminine at all.

Then he took off the wig and dropped it onto the floor. His eyes scorched me. He looked like a pirate who'd just found buried treasure.

I swallowed, nervous but not ready to run. His finger stroked down my belly, then farther until it started teasing that little part of me that he'd pleasured so well before. I melted for him.

The last thing I remember is the gleam in his eyes before his head bent down to me. His tongue started playing with me down there, spending more time and energy than he had on my mouth. I felt a sharp bite on my thigh just before I climaxed yet again. . . .

Later that night, he taught me a few more things, such as how to suck a man like a candy cane. It was fun, like finding peppermint candy, hot and red and spicy, under those fancy skirts of his. . . .

What do you mean, how do you suck a man like that? Lordy, Joan, I thought you've tried almost everything by now. Let's see now; how can I explain it?

Jean-Marie and I were lying on the bed together, with his arms wrapped around me. We'd gotten rid of the peppermint-pink dress because the wool rubbed my skin. Now his petticoat's crinolines scratched my legs. I twitched restlessly and tried to move away. Then I just sat up and told him to take it off. His mouth quirked at my tone but he stood up and stripped the wretched thing over his head. My jaw dropped as I looked at my first naked man.

Do you remember that statue of David that we saw

in Florence? Not the big marble one by Michelangelo but the elegant bronze one? David as a beautiful youth, with a winged helmet? Recall how you teased me for staring at it for so long and coming back the next day to see it again? Jean-Marie's body was like that, slim and muscular. Creamy white, unlike the bronze, but deep red where his cock jutted toward me.

I touched it carefully with just the tip of my finger. He jerked slightly and hissed softly but didn't step away. I swirled my finger around the tip, which was an even darker shade of scarlet, and felt its wetness. I tasted my finger and he groaned my name.

I wanted to sample more of him so I leaned forward and licked up the thick hard shaft. My tongue bobbed as it came to the fat head and I twisted slightly so I could explore the other side, before returning to the start. Jean-Marie said my name again hoarsely and his hands gripped my hair.

I did it again but this time, Jean-Marie's hands directed my head as I swirled my tongue over him. Jean-Marie continued to guide me, curving my tongue around, over and down his scarlet shaft. I remembered sucking candy canes, how I followed a red stripe around the long shaft, then up and over the top, before sweeping back around to the base. I tried that motion on him and he growled approval, his hands tightening in my hair.

I did it again and again, enjoying how he began to rock under my mouth. My hands came up and echoed my tongue's movements. Heat built under my attentions and I tasted his own sweet spice, better than anything I'd ever found in a Christmas stocking.

His body jerked harder and faster as I sucked him. The rhythm reminded me of how my hips danced beneath his tongue. Then he tensed and shuddered. I lifted my head and watched thick white drops pulse out from the head of his cock. His cream flowed down his crimson shaft, red and white together like peppermint candy. . . .

Well, what else do you want to know, Joan?

That night was when I fell in love with the law and the people who'd made it. The final went well, even though I was still bleeding a bit from that bite on my thigh. I found a new boardinghouse for the second semester and things got better at the University.

Occasionally, my thigh will start burning under a full moon and I'll feel a little trickle of blood running down. Then I'll go to the library and browse through the stacks, hoping to hear a French voice talking about the founding fathers. . . .

thirtieth birthday

a tale of ethan templeton

I've been working on a grandfather's book of memories, which makes me feel ancient. The cowboy told me that I would remember but I could only speak of it once. So I am writing this now, while I can still recall the details, just to prove to myself that even a tenured professor of mathematics and his wife were young and crazy once.

I was on sabbatical in Austin for my thirtieth birthday. Carol and the kids were doing well there but I felt old. Carol still looked like the crazy blonde I'd fallen in love with but I looked much the same then as I do now—as I did when I was eighteen: a nerd. Brown eyes, brown hair going bald, glasses. At least I still swam enough to have a decent build.

Carol really surprised me that year for my birthday. She gave me a certificate good for one fantasy of my choice. We'd talked about it long enough that she knew which one I'd choose: seeing another man make love to her. I wanted John Travolta in *Urban Cowboy*, she wanted Frank Langella in *Dracula*.

Carol found a baby-sitter for my birthday weekend and we were free.

We drove around that Saturday to a lot of different roadhouses, looking for just the right cowboy. We started at the trendy roadhouses and watched dozens of urban cowboys two-step across the floor.

Too fake, said Carol.

We tried other roadhouses, looking for real cowboys. Men who could wrestle a steer or ride a woman. The roadhouses got dirtier and raunchier as we hunted. We started seeing drunks and bouncers more often than dancers.

Too sloppy, I said.

We wound up after midnight at a roadhouse in the Texas Hill Country under the full moon. We found a table by the wall and looked around while sipping some surprisingly good beer.

We couldn't see much of the band. The lighting was too bad and they were sheltered behind chicken wire. A few couples were swaying across the floor to some Western swing. Most of the action was at the bar, where men were holding forth over beer and eyeing the available women. They were real cowboys, with scuffed boots and easy drawls.

One man really drew my attention. He was tall and blond, slender but muscled, with a dusty Stetson pulled down over his face. He leaned back against the bar, watching the room like a bored jaguar surveying the wild pig population in Honduras.

He looked like just the man I'd always dreamed of being. I wanted to see his reaction to Carol. I wanted to see him get hot when he saw my little blonde wife. I wanted to hear her moan when he tugged her nipples. I wanted . . .

I glanced at Carol. She was watching him too. Our eyes met and she nodded, slowly then emphatically. I stood up and went over to him.

His eyes were very cold while I explained what I wanted. He studied Carol while I talked then looked back at me after I finished. He scrutinized me as thoroughly as he'd watched her, and I flushed. His hazel eyes flickered down to my crotch. Blood was gathering there, as it had done since I first saw him. I blushed harder but stood my ground.

He agreed to make love to her on one condition: that he'd get to bite each of us. That was easier to agree to than some of the things we'd imagined.

Carol led the way out of the door with him following right behind. She jumped a bit when his hand went down the back of her jeans but recovered quickly.

We walked across the parking lot to a little motel. I went inside to get a room, while they waited. I came back to find Carol leaning against a car, his hat on her head and her shirt open to his kisses. Her eyes were half-shut as she fondled his shoulders. I could hear his wet mouth moving across her skin and the way she choked and gasped as he worked.

An old bed with a sagging mattress took up most of the motel room. A small table and a narrow chair were the only other furniture. He jerked his head at the chair and I sat in it.

He kissed Carol long and slow, holding her so that I could observe all of her response. His sharp white teeth gleamed when he sucked on her lip. He caressed her thoroughly, rousing her then backing off, always making sure that I could see. It was better than any movie.

I moaned once, when his mouth drew out her nipple until it popped free. He glanced at me and I bit my lip. His look promised retribution if I disturbed them again.

He leisurely stripped off Carol's clothes. I saw the

sweat running down her as I felt my cock start to drip. He laid her across the bed and knelt on the floor, her legs hanging over his shoulders. His fingers worked her and then his mouth. I watched hungrily, my hand on my cock echoing his movements.

I tried to time myself to match their climax but he was taking too long. I tried to hold myself back but I could see her cream dripping and hear the bed as she rode his face. He lifted her hips higher and worked her ass. The bed's rattles started to drown out her sobs as she begged him for more.

I shuddered when his tongue disappeared into her back entrance. I felt pressure deep within me as my body demanded completion. I must have made a noise because he looked at me again.

His green eyes stopped that surge and I froze, like a gazelle under a lion's eyes. Carol whimpered but he still watched me, silently ordering me to wait. I slowly lifted my hands and placed them on the chair's arms. He studied me a minute longer and then went back to Carol.

I clenched the chair until my knuckles turned white as I watched him build Carol up. He finished her with his fingers deep inside her, driving her body across the bed. He bit her thigh and sucked her. Scarlet beads fell slowly to the worn carpet. I closed my eyes as she screamed how good it was. . . .

"*Behind her,*" a voice said in my head. "*Get behind her now.*"

Who is that? my mind bleated.

"*You know who it is.*" The cold voice carried the cowboy's implacability. "*Move. Now.*"

My body obeyed him while my thoughts tumbled over each other. I opened my eyes to see his tongue flicker as it followed a crimson trail toward her knee. Carol's arms were flung over her head, arching her beautiful breasts with their pink nipples to the ceiling.

I climbed on the bed behind her so she lay between my legs, her head resting on my lap. My hands found their way to her breasts, plumping them and stretching out the nipples. She purred like a kitten and rubbed against me.

He stood up easily and stretched. Then he casually gathered Carol's hips and lifted them, rubbing his shaft's fat tip through her creamy folds. Carol groaned and writhed, begging him to finish her. He entered her slowly, varying his angle and depth and speed, while she strung four-letter words together into a mantra.

I could see every move they made as he pleasured her. I ached with frustration and excitement.

He lifted Carol off the bed and held her against his chest. I stared at them, startled.

"Lie down."

I obeyed quickly, unwilling to cross him again. Then he brought Carol over my hips and held her there, where I could see every detail of her enjoyment. White and red drops gleamed on her golden thatch. He slowly lowered her, while I avidly watched my shaft disappear into her.

Carol braced herself on her knees as she settled fully onto me.

"Wait."

I bit my lip, willing myself not to climax. I saw him leave her and walk around the bed toward me with a gunfighter's deliberate stroll.

Then she began to ride me, using me as she chose and as she had never done before. I memorized every bounce of her rosy breasts and every toss of her bright hair as she moved, slowly at first but gradually faster. Her thighs slapped against my hips as she chanted my name in rhythm with her thrusts.

I fell back, my body bowing as it centered under her. Her cunt clenched me as her climax grabbed her. She threw her head back and shouted my name, grinding her golden thatch into my dark fur.

"Now."

I arched as cream burst from me and the vampire fed from my neck for the first time. . . .

What do I remember most? Once I licked Carol's breasts like an ice-cream sundae, while he rode Carol and she gasped encouragement to both of us.

Or was it when I licked his cream out of Carol's cunt while he probed her asshole with his tongue and she purred above our heads?

Once Carol lay on my stomach while he bit and licked her back, catching every drop of sweat and blood. She twisted and moaned under his attentions, her nipples stabbing at my chest.

Another time, Carol sprawled across the bed, boneless and exhausted. We both still sought her out; my mouth explored every inch of her feet as I tasted and sucked them. I paused frequently to watch his tongue clean her hidden folds while his fingers dallied with her asshole.

Once Carol sucked his shaft like a dog working a bone when I took her from behind. I bit my lip when she rolled her hips eagerly against me. The blood dripped slowly down before I remembered to lick it away. I was glad no one at the university could see me.

But mostly I remember feeding him our blood, opening myself to him, while Carol helped him drink from me, or helping him feed from her. Yielding to his demands heightened our sexual frenzy. Our bodies oozed scarlet drops from his bites. Blood stained the bed and scented the room.

His hand toyed with Carol while he fed from my thigh for the last time. She'd lost her voice and I'd lost my glasses sometime during the night. Her eyes were shut as she idly fondled my bruised cock in rhythm with his fingers' motion.

She shifted and I whimpered when she lifted her hand. She rolled me from my side to my back and kneeled above my head. I hummed approval as her cunt settled over my mouth. I happily drowned in her while she sighed in ecstasy and his mouth returned to my thigh.

He finally let us lose consciousness as first light flickered behind the grimy curtains. I slept a long time, waking to Carol's concern. We both had bruises and sore muscles in intimate places. But the bite marks faded within a week. . . .

Sometimes, when the Detroit winter is long and cold, my neck itches under a full moon. Then Carol and I both look south and remember, and almost wish to be thirty again.

the morning after

a tale of don rafael perez,
ethan templeton, and jean-marie st. just

Liz yawned her way into the breakfast nook and dropped into a chair. Becca eyed her over a mug of steaming black coffee then stood up. She put down a fresh mug of coffee in front of Liz and then resumed her own study of the coffee's potential.

"Thanks," Liz offered. She cupped her hands around the fragrant brew. "Thank God for coffee, especially after nights like that."

"Amen," Becca responded and took a deep drink.

Julie appeared in the doorway, somehow managing to look like a supermodel in her scruffy Miami Dolphins jersey. Her face lacked makeup and her blonde hair was finding new ways to defy gravity. She was still the most beautiful woman in the room.

Becca sighed into her coffee. Julie was also the sweetest girl in the room. She even had a knack for matchmaking. Becca shuddered over her two divorces, both from men that Julie hadn't liked. Next time she'd listen to Julie.

"Anybody need a warm-up?" Julie asked, holding the coffeepot up.

"I do," Becca answered. She got out of her chair, wincing as muscles protested last night's hard use. She hoped her steps weren't as loose-limbed as the other girls' but suspected they were. It had been quite a party.

Liz finished stirring her usual flood of cream and sugar into her mug and sniffed it cautiously. "Perfect," she muttered and took a deep swallow.

Becca and Julie's eyes met over Liz's head. Liz never bothered with calorie counting like the other girls. She was still as much of a tomboy as she'd been at twelve when they'd all met. But her athletic skills kept her figure trim and her skin freckled, a nice anchor for her dark eyes, brunette hair, and big smile. She often complained that men always treated her like a kid sister and never had any serious intentions.

Becca thought about adding cream to her coffee and then decided against it. She spent too much time in the gym now, trying to keep her curves on the slender side rather than the pleasingly plump side. Men liked her honey-blonde looks and curves, almost as much as they liked her family's money.

"Have a good time last night?" Becca asked the room in general.

"Great Halloween party!" Julie enthused. "You were right. I had a much better time here than I would have in New York. And that Frenchman. Ooh, baby!" She kissed her fingers in salute.

Liz and Becca stared at her.

"Tall guy? Dressed as the Phantom of the Opera?" Liz asked.

"That's the one. Jean-Marie St. Just."

"But, Julie darling, you barely reached his chest."

"So what? And let me tell you," Julie smiled reminiscently as she licked a milky mustache from her upper lip, "he knew clothing too. Recognized my dressmaker immediately and said some wonderful things about my gown's bias cut. He was almost enough to make me move back to Texas permanently."

Liz and Becca looked at each other in shock. Understanding each other completely, they immersed themselves in coffee-drinking again. Coffee was something they could handle, unlike Julie talking about moving home.

"What about you, darlings?" Julie asked. "Your vampire was a real hunk, Becca. Rafael Perez, right? He looked damn good next to your Morticia Addams outfit. Rather large for your typical Latin lover but who cares with that body?"

Becca remembered seeing Rafael's shoulders looming above her as he thrust into her. Was that the second or third time he rode her? The aches deep down in her body said that he'd had her more times than that. She blushed all the way down to her chest.

She opened her mouth to say something but an iron vise clamped around her throat. She remembered a deep voice forbidding her to ever speak of what they'd done together. She took a deep breath and relaxed slowly, as the ban faded with her decision not to talk.

"So he was that good after you two went upstairs. Good for you, darling." Julie lifted her coffee mug in salute.

Then she and Becca turned their attention to Liz, who kept her face buried in the enormous mug.

"I saw you, Liz, with that tall rebel officer. Nice, nice butt there. Didn't seem to be eyeing you like a sister," Julie teased. "What was his name, Becca?"

"Pete introduced him as Ethan Templeton. Come on, Liz, tell us about it," Becca urged, glad to turn attention from herself. "Blond guys don't come along every day who look like a mountain lion on the prowl. Especially fellows who match your *Gone with the Wind* finery. Did he roar in the bedroom? Or were you the one doing the roaring?"

"I don't remember," Liz managed before grabbing another gulp of coffee.

Julie's eyebrows went up. "I swear I heard you giggling for a solid five minutes in there, Liz. Right after the bed stopped pounding the wall."

Liz shrugged. Her oversized T-shirt fell away from her neck, revealing a substantial hickey.

Becca whistled. "Sounds like we all had a good time last night. I think this needs a special salute."

She unearthed a bottle of Kahlua and poured a dollop into each mug. The three friends clinked their mugs together and drank.

"Halloween, and I met a vampire," Becca mused.

"Jean-Marie said he was a vampire but I just laughed at him. That costume was definitely for the Phantom."

"Ethan mentioned something about being a vampire, while we were dancing," Liz offered. "He did leave before dawn."

"That's when Rafael left."

"And Jean-Marie. He said his fangs were real, too."

The three women looked at each other.

"Could it be?" Liz started.

"Nah."

"Definitely not," confirmed Becca.

Each woman took another drink and resolved never to mention the bite marks on their thighs to another. After all, a guy could be kinky without being a vampire.

And there's no such thing as vampires, even on the morning after Halloween.

spotlight
a tale of don rafael perez

TO: ritacat@nyc . . .
FROM: brynda@austn . . .
DATE: Mon,
SUBJECT: Scenery

Thanks for the care package! It was waiting for me when I got home tonight. You can find a lot of things down here in Texas, some of them damn good like the cowboys. But nothing really compares to a genuine kosher pickle from Brooklyn.

I'm still working temp, always as a paralegal so the

money's pretty good. Moving from assignment to assignment keeps me from getting bored. And yes, it also keeps me busy enough that I don't think about Dave all the time.

No, I'm not coming back to Brooklyn, no matter how often you ask or tempt me with talk of clearance sales in the garment district! I'd rather stay in Texas where we were happiest. Okay, I did move to Austin but that was to avoid reminders of the Navy.

What's your next question? Scenery? Hell, you always ask about the masculine scenery but today I've finally got some to report.

I was trying to decipher Mrs. Garrity's chicken scratches (she calls them corrections) on some filings this afternoon. Suddenly Pete Tompkins's nasal whine echoed down the hallways as he escorted a group of men into his office. His words surprised me since he was being obsequious rather than an arrogant jerk. So I looked up fast, just to see who had humbled him.

Pete had three men with him. I can't tell you much about two of them except they were probably lawyers, given his usual visitors.

But the third man knocked my socks off. Big man, well over six feet, built like a linebacker, black hair, dark eyes, olive skin, nasty scar on his forehead. He was wearing a classic western suit, white shirt, and Stetson so crisp that they almost looked like formal wear. He prowled down that corridor like Wayne Gretzky heading for the goal—graceful and quiet and dangerous.

They passed me by and I turned to openly stare like everyone else.

Rita, he had the finest ass I have ever seen. Hard and solid, with a beautiful rippling flow of muscle. I drooled. My mouth hung open far enough to catch flies. Some distant part of my brain considered the width of his shoulders and the strength of his thighs. But my hormones went screaming after his ass like a cop chasing a bank robber and daydreams of promotions.

Lily and I talked about the visitors for half an hour in the washroom but we made sure to be back in our cubicles before they left. Thank heavens for low walls on cubicles: I could get a really good view without being too obvious.

Let me tell you, the front half of that man was fine. Gorgeous chest and yeah, a very masculine bulge inside those pants. His eyes met mine and I blushed scarlet but I didn't look away. His mouth quirked before Pete regained his attention.

If I wrote down even half of my fantasies about what I could do with that man, the office email system would melt down. Let me just say that I retired to the ladies' room to enjoy them and returned to my cubicle as a very relaxed woman.

I'm feeling good enough now that I plan to go out this evening. There's an open mike every Monday and Tuesday night at a listening club I've heard of. I'll wear that great outfit you sent me from Bloomie's.

Dear Rita:

I had planned to send an email about last night but I'm not brave enough to talk about it over the Internet. So you'll just have to put up with a low-tech account sent via snail mail.

The listening club was just the way I'd pictured it. It's an old packing shed next to the railroad tracks and is famous as the first desegregated club in Austin. (Although Lily says it always served both blacks and whites so how could it be desegregated?) It's a lot cleaner than expected, especially in that neighborhood.

The inside, though, has a pool hall, a DJ's station with some of the fanciest electronics I've ever seen, a gift shop, a small saloon, and the best listening room I've ever been in. Nothing fancy, mind, but efficient, comfortable, and almost perfect acoustics. I found a seat in the rear, paid for my soda, and settled back to enjoy.

This open mike session provided some good examples of why Austin is called the Capitol of Live Music. I listened happily to some great jazz, a couple of operatic arias, and a lot of folk music.

By eleven, I was yawning and thinking about going to work the next day. Only a handful of people remained when the MC announced that the next act would be the last of the evening.

My eyes almost fell out of my skull when I saw who the last act was: the Spanish gentleman who'd humbled Pete Tompkins. Now he was wearing a cowboy's uniform, with a long-sleeved starched white shirt, starched blue jeans, and cowboy boots. He had a beautiful acoustic guitar that he carried like an old friend.

I immediately abandoned my unobtrusive seat and found a place in front of the stage.

He sang something haunting in Spanish, his fingers caressing the guitar like a beautiful woman. His voice was rich and deep, lingering over the liquid syllables and roughening occasionally for emphasis. His chocolate-brown eyes were half-veiled by the longest lashes I've ever seen as he sang of love lost and hope gone.

I wanted to be that guitar so much that every ripple of his fingers across the strings made me tremble. I squirmed when he finished, realizing just how much dampness he'd called forth from between my thighs. My face was flushed and my breasts ached, hungry for his touch, desperate to comfort him.

I applauded, of course, like everyone else there. He smiled at us and his eyes met mine for a moment. His eyebrow lifted and I blushed like a virgin.

"*Gracias, amigos.* Now for something livelier, to send us all home." He played a fandango, a lively old dance tune that soon had us clapping our hands and stomping our feet. His music filled the hall and we rose with it, swaying to the infectious beat.

Somehow the rhythm stayed with us as we filed out, still humming the song. My parking spot was blocked by a big pickup truck so I had time to start thinking. About what I really wanted . . . and needed.

Finally I got out and went back into the club.

He was standing in the pool hall, talking to the owner, when I came in. Both of them nodded to me but, hell, I was only interested in the musician.

"I just wanted to say thank you for the marvelous performance. You're a great guitarist," I began. I had to say something respectable, no matter how much my body longed to be fondled by him.

His eyes searched mine, hot and intent for an answer

to the oldest question of all between a man and a woman. Heat flowed down my spine and I must have nodded.

"*Gracias*, señora. You are very kind." His hand slipped under my elbow, strong and warm. "Please excuse us, Gary." He steered me back toward the small saloon, which was empty and dark.

I started to chatter immediately, of course, as you might guess. "I've never heard anything like that first song you played. It sounded old, perhaps seventeenth century. My professor always said . . ."

He flipped open the light panel. One touch brought a single spotlight up on the saloon's tiny stage and the single stool on it but left the rest of room touched with shadows. The door swung shut behind us and the room darkened further, making the single light seem even brighter.

I kept talking, nervous as hell at being this close to a man for the first time since Dave's death.

"Uh, my professor said . . ."

"Do you always talk this much, señora?" His voice was whisky and velvet after my jerky words. His finger lightly caressed my cheek and I trembled.

"Uh, yes," I admitted.

"Then perhaps we can find other uses for your sweet

mouth." He tilted his head and I stayed quite still, my mouth still hanging open. His tongue teased my lips; I must have sighed. He chuckled softly and sucked my lip delicately. I slid my hands up his arms for support as a shaft of need raced through me.

Then his mouth claimed me and I stopped thinking. He kissed like an angel, a swirl of masculine tastes and textures as our mouths learned every detail of the other. I pressed closer to him as his tongue explored me, shuddering when his big hand rubbed my ass. I stopped thinking and just enjoyed. Shit, he was good.

I regained my senses somewhat when he settled me on the stool. I found myself on the stage, seated like a star performer in the spotlight, while he tweaked my skirts back into respectability. I shivered at the contact and tried to think.

A door closed, somewhere in the distance. "What's that?"

"Gary's departure." His voice was abstracted, then his eyes met mine again. He smiled slowly and my pulse started to race. "We're alone now, señora. Do you wish to leave?"

"No." I was very certain about that much at least. I was far too hungry for this man to walk away now.

"Bien." His mouth claimed mine again and I forgot my qualms, such as they were. His big hands cupped my

breasts through the thin shirt, kneading and petting them until I swayed and moaned in Anglo-Saxon as my nipples hardened. "Do you like my touch?"

"Yes, of course, you idiot."

"Then show me."

I blinked at the rasp in his voice and stared up at him. Hunger had tightened his mouth and brought color to his high cheekbones. "Señora," he warned me softly.

I slipped the first button free slowly and his eyes flashed. The second button was easier and the third easiest of all when he swallowed hard. I took a deep breath and let the shirt fall open.

"Beautiful," he growled and lifted my breasts in his hands. He weighed them and brushed his thumb over first one nipple, then the other. I shuddered and closed my eyes as the rough caress burned down to my belly. I was so very damp between my legs. Oh, fuck.

Then he put his mouth to work. He licked and suckled until every inch of my chest understood that pleasure came from him. I braced my hands behind me on the stool and arched my back, the better to open myself to him. I trembled and wriggled and moaned in delight at his attentions.

And I talked too, of course, using Brooklyn terms and language Dave had taught me. About how damn good he felt, and couldn't he do the same thing on the other side, and thanked him when he did as I asked . . .

And I sobbed when his hands traveled up the inside of my legs, under my skirt. He had wicked hands that knew exactly how to stroke and fondle and coax yet more cream from my cunt.

"*Nieve y rosas,*" he murmured. Then his voice strengthened. "Lift your hips."

"What the fuck?" I tried to open my eyes. Thinking was very low on my list of priorities at that moment, especially when a man had just compared me to snow and roses.

"Don't think, señora," he coaxed. "Live for today, not yesterday."

My eyes met his for a moment and I saw how truly he understood my grief. My eyes slid away from his, unwilling to reveal too much of myself. Oh, crap.

"Señora," he growled softly and a jolt of lust ran through me. I took a deep breath then raised my hips. He rolled my skirt up to my waist and cold air touched my very heated skin, making me shiver. I stared up at him, speechless for once, as my panties slipped away in his grasp.

"*Bien.* Now spread your legs very widely." His hands guided me. "Wider still, señora. *Perfecto.*"

I must have looked like a monument to lust under

that spotlight with my shirt hanging off my shoulders and my skirt reduced to a belt. Breasts flushed and hard with nipples pointed and red, my lips swollen. "What the hell are you going to do?" I asked inanely, as if I cared what he did as long as he did it soon.

He chuckled, his eyes dancing with laughter. "Guess, señora." Then he dropped to his knees before me.

I stared down at his dark head and reverted to my mother's vocabulary. "Ohmygawd."

And if I'd thought he was talented before, when he taught new meanings of pleasure to my mouth and breasts, I knew he was a genius as soon as he tasted my cunt. He explored my nether lips like a man intent on learning every detail of a fabulous landscape. His tongue swirled through my folds, finding every drop of cream and coaxing out more. He lifted his head and licked his lips as he caught my eyes.

"*Dulce con miel*," he approved and I blushed scarlet. He smiled wickedly, his dark eyes hot as fine whisky, then returned to tasting me. He played a flamenco rhythm on my aching flesh that kept me poised and trembling, frantic for more. I writhed under him, fighting to be closer, more turned on than if I'd been using my vibrator.

And I talked the whole time, praising him and thanking him and asking for just a little more . . .

Until I was begging him for the orgasm that hung so close and yet so infuriatingly far away. "Goddammit, I'll do anything! Just finish me!"

"*Es verdad?*" he drawled, lifting his head slightly to watch his blunt finger tease me. My thighs tightened desperately.

"Yes, damn you, anything!"

"*Bien,*" he purred and brought his poet's mouth back to me. Before I could complain once more, he bit my thighs, bringing a momentary touch of pain, then flicked his thumb skillfully over my clit.

I screamed and shattered into a thousand satisfied pieces as he tasted my blood for the first time.

I don't really know what else to tell you, Rita. All the other climaxes I had with his head between my thighs? Or how he stretched me with three fingers then taught my insides some new ways to climax?

Or of digging my fingers into his magnificent ass, feeling it flex so he could better drive that splendid cock deeper into me? And how every pulse that carried my blood into his mouth only seemed to deepen my pleasure.

He said I could speak of our encounter once. But I'm afraid I'll forget what he was like if I tell you.

So maybe I'll just tear up this letter and keep my memories for myself.

TO: ritacat@nyc . . .
FROM: brynda@austn . . .
DATE: Thu,
SUBJECT: Dating in Austin

Yup, the listening club really did have some good musicians. No, I didn't go out with any of them afterward. I'm just not ready to get involved with a man on a regular basis so it's best to stay away.

I've decided to take a steady job so I'll be starting at a local law firm next week. They specialize in real estate and their largest client is the Santiago Trust, a big trust that's been around since before the Civil War. I'm really looking forward to it as a good opportunity to use my training.

The only disadvantage is that I don't believe in mixing business with pleasure. One of their clients is that big Spaniard, the one with the best ass in the world. Obviously it would be unprofessional to sleep with him but maybe a little oral sex would be okay.

What do you think?

bourbon with a splash

a tale of ethan templeton

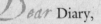

ear Diary,

I can't believe I just wrote those words. I swore I wouldn't be like every other little girl and that included keeping a diary. But, hell, if it's the only way to remember Ethan, then I'll do it.

Of course, there's a lot of things I swore I'd never do, most of which I have managed to try. I still haven't gotten drunk on bourbon, though.

Ethan has given me permission to talk once about my meetings with him. I told my girlfriends about our first meeting and haven't been able to tell anyone else about it since. I can't even write it down, dammit. So from now on, I'm keeping a log of all of our meetings. I probably won't be able to show this log to anyone but who cares? At least I can read it.

I met Ethan while I was a cop in a suburb of Austin, Texas, before I joined the metro police. Damn, now I can feel that block against writing down how we met. So let's just say that we met and had some really great sex. That's pretty rare for me; most guys are too scared to approach a gal who can bench press more than she weighs, is rated expert with pistol and rifle, third-degree black belt in karate and always carries handcuffs.

Wimps.

But that didn't bother Ethan at all, boy howdy! So we started seeing each other, fairly often but not regularly. It's never been a boyfriend-girlfriend kind of arrangement.

Hell, who'd try that with a vampire? I'm certainly not going for an exclusive relationship with him. He'd immediately say no and I'd sure like to find an ordinary guy for marriage one day. But in the meantime, you can't find a better partner for blowing off steam than Ethan. More than once, he's also provided damn useful information on some very bad-ass dudes, which saved the day for me and my fellow cops—and the public. (I'm not going to say anything more than that, even in my own diary. His information has always been good as gold and I've never paid a penny for it. What my supervisors don't have to legally know won't hurt 'em.)

I always wanted to be a Texas Ranger and finally, the Texas DPS accepted my application, a required step before becoming a Ranger. (Yes! I'm still pumped up about that news.) So I worked out my notice at metro police and arranged to take some time off before starting as a state trooper. I had a list of things to accomplish and Ethan was the key to one of them. So I called and left a voice mail for him. (It always fascinates me that a guy born in 1839 is so comfortable with modern technology.)

He called me back on my cell phone later that night, while I was having a cup of coffee and a doughnut in my cruiser. I recognized his number immediately on the readout.

"Hi, Ethan," I mumbled through a mouthful of doughnut.

He snorted. I'm always eating when he calls me. Hell, I can't help it if I have to consume twice as much as anyone else just to keep up my weight.

"What can I do for you, Steve?"

It's usually best to skip small talk with Ethan, which is fine by me. I'm not much of one for polite chit-chat, either.

"My last day with the department is Friday and I'm spending next week with my folks, but I don't have to be there until Sunday night. Care to do something on Saturday night?"

"Sure," he agreed. Then he asked me the question I was afraid of. The one that I'd have to answer because it's always best to tell him the truth, no matter how embarrassing. "Got anything in mind?"

"Uh, well, I was wondering," I stuttered. "I'd like to just feel like a woman. Your woman."

The line went silent. I waited, without a thought of my hot coffee or doughnut.

"Doing anything I want, Stephanie Amanda?" he purred. I broke out into a sweat at the way he wrapped that drawl around all the syllables of my name. I didn't even flinch at the sound of my all too-frilly middle name. "Just want to be feminine? Got some fantasies about being submissive? Maybe try some rough stuff?"

"Yeah," I agreed. The heat had moved down my body at his suggestions. Now, more than my brow was damp. "Something like that."

"Okay. Get a room at the Sleepytime Motel for Saturday night. I'll pick you up there at eight."

"Fine." I'd never seen a room at the Sleepytime Motel except during a bust. One thing for sure, nobody there would blink at anything he wanted to do.

"I'll send you some clothes. Be sure you're wearing those and nothing else when I pick you up." His voice was harsher now.

"Okay," I managed. I pressed my knees together against my body's response. He'd never ordered me around before. Hell, I was usually the one doing that to him and he obviously liked it. I was surprised that I enjoyed him bossing me around because I've never been called meek.

"And Stephanie? Make sure you shave that pussy of yours. My woman doesn't hide anything from me."

I choked on a sip of coffee. Shave? Down there? But even if my mind wasn't sure, my body was convinced that this was a very good idea. I closed my eyes against another surge of wetness between my legs. I might have to jack off before going back on duty after this break.

"Roger that," I got out, unconsciously using the catch phrase from work.

Ethan laughed.

"See you Saturday." He hung up. I sat in my cruiser for a moment and then got out resignedly. I could use the doughnut shop's restroom for some privacy while I dealt with my reactions.

The rest of the week went past in a fairly normal way. At least the events were normal; my mind kept running off for daydreams about Ethan's plans. I took a lot of teasing for thinking about my next job. The department gave me a great sendoff on Friday night and I managed not to get too drunk. I didn't want to be hungover on Saturday.

I checked into the Sleepytime Motel at five on Saturday and found a hefty package waiting for me. I took a room at the back; every cop in town knew my Mustang convertible and I didn't want to advertise my presence here.

I opened it as soon as I got into the room, of course. My jaw dropped at the mountain of brown suede that emerged. Leather chaps, fringed leather jacket, cowboy boots. They looked more like working duds than dress-up attire and were beautifully made. I petted them, enjoying the smooth velvety feel, and held them up to see how they'd fit. The jacket reached mid-thigh, longer than most of that style.

Then I started hunting for the rest of my clothes. Even Ethan wouldn't want me to wear just chaps and a jacket, right? I shook everything out three or four times but couldn't find a scrap of anything else, not even socks.

I called down to the desk and they swore there was nothing else waiting for me. I even searched the office myself without finding anything. (Well, that's not quite accurate. They were running a heck of a pool on the coming high school football season. I ignored that, since I wasn't a cop at the moment.)

Finally, I let myself back into my room and stared at the clothing spread out on the bed. Jacket, chaps, boots. That rig didn't hide anything, except maybe my toes. I cursed my own stupidity at not setting stricter rules when I'd had the chance. Then I shrugged. I was sure that Ethan wouldn't harm me, even when he drank my blood. Besides, my body kept celebrating the possibilities of that clothing.

So I gathered my toiletries together and went into the surprisingly clean bathroom. A long, hot bath did wonders for my frame of mind. After I'd toweled off, I arranged the hand mirrors I'd remembered to bring and started trimming my bush with the sharpest pair of barber's scissors I could find. A big dollop of shaving cream followed and then I started to shave. Carefully, of course. Very, very carefully.

The results startled me. I looked naked and felt much more on display than I ever had before, even in the women's showers at the gym or the station. I could feel every breath of air, every little twitch of my thighs. I could also see very clearly exactly what my excitement looked like, my folds deep red and beaded with moisture like an exotic flower.

I looked at my face in the mirror and almost didn't recognize myself. My grandma was a Cherokee out of Oklahoma and I have something of her look. Well, it was an exotic female I faced, someone I'd never seen before: big brown eyes set slightly aslant, pupils huge and drowsy with lust. A hectic flush of color on my cheekbones meant that I didn't need any makeup, not that I usually wore any. My mouth was red and ripe, trembling a little, as if it needed to be kissed.

Then I caught sight of the clock's reflection: seven something. I turned around and cursed; I had less than fifteen minutes to finish getting ready. I put on a little makeup, nothing fancy, just lipstick and mascara, something to celebrate a hot date.

I pulled on the leathers as fast as possible. They fit perfectly, of course; Ethan isn't one to get anything wrong.

That left me with three minutes to see how I looked. The jacket covered me well enough so that I looked like a cowgirl in working clothes. At least while I stood up straight and kept everything in place.

But if the jacket was unbuttoned or removed, then I looked like a sexual toy. The chaps outlined my privates like an engraved invitation. I could see everything I had, especially with the hair gone.

If I bent over, the jacket slid up and out of the way, leaving my butt begging for attention.

I bit my lip when I thought of how Ethan might respond to that opportunity.

The doorbell rang while I was still working on ways to stay decent with the jacket. I froze at the sound and took a deep breath. Eight o'clock exactly.

I opened the door immediately, not needing to check who was there. Ethan looked down at me, hazel eyes noting every detail of my appearance.

"Aren't you going to greet me, Stephanie?" he drawled.

I flushed and reached up to do so, the jacket riding up over my hips with the movement. His lips were cool and hard but quickly warmed up. Soon he was doing the kissing and I was moaning into his mouth. Part of my brain knew that his hands were busy on my bare skin under the jacket but most of me didn't care what he did, as long as he kept doing it.

Ethan broke off the kiss finally and I laid my forehead against his chest.

"Unbutton the jacket, Stephanie."

I shook my head to clear it and stepped away from him. He came into the room and closed the door, then leaned casually against it. He was dressed in black leather from head to toe, like a tough motorcycle rider. The leathers emphasized his body's perfection and set off his blond good looks perfectly. Their rich smell made my mouth water, as if the sight of him wasn't enough. I suddenly understood a lot more about folks with a leather fetish than I ever had before.

"Stephanie." His voice was sharp and I shook myself into movement. I started to unbutton my jacket but hesitated at what it would reveal. I saw the stern look in his eyes; dammit, he didn't look aroused at all. Just forbidding, like exam day from the strictest teacher in high school. I finished unbuttoning it and stopped, instinctively waiting for his next command. I was also nervous as hell about stripping off for him.

"Take it off and lay it on the chair."

I obeyed and turned back to face him. I kept my hands firmly at my sides, not letting them stray to cover me. Ethan had always liked my breasts, inherited from my German grandmother. I knew they'd be too much for my hands to cover, especially if I also tried to conceal my crotch.

I closed my eyes and tried to fight back my blush. Undressing just before you jump into bed is one thing. Exposing yourself at the beginning of the evening is quite another. Maybe it would have been easier if I'd broken my old rule and gotten drunk on bourbon.

"Kneel over the bed and spread yourself wide so I can see how well you shaved."

My legs were stiff and uncooperative as I went to the bed, giving him a long glance over my shoulder. I wanted to scream at him to do something, not just look. But I obeyed and waited for the next command.

I didn't hear him move, just felt the first blunt finger trail through my folds. I jerked in surprise and then twitched when he stroked me back and forth, just the way I like it. Slow and steady, not a direct attack on my clit. Problem was that my clit was more than willing for an immediate assault. I whimpered and circled my hips, begging for more action.

"Hold still," he snapped. I stopped, lashed by the sharp order, and waited.

"Dammit, Ethan," I started to say.

Two fingers played with me now. I bit my lip at the knowing touch, trying to stay passive.

"Nice job of shaving," Ethan remarked. I moaned when his thumb circled my asshole, an attention that I always enjoyed. I'd even flushed myself out there, hoping to encourage him. I felt the first shimmers of climax and started to let go of myself in preparation.

His hands left me abruptly and I cursed at the interruption. Ethan slapped my ass hard and I jumped. "What the hell?"

"Tonight you're my woman, Stephanie. Everything

about you is mine, including your orgasms. So you don't come until I tell you to. And you never argue about anything I do."

His slow drawl was more commanding than a barked order by my former sergeant. My body was still more than willing to play but my brain started wondering what the heck I'd let myself in for.

"Looks like it's time for your first lesson about who's boss."

My treacherous body trembled, obviously willing for any instruction he cared to give.

He sat down beside me and smacked my ass casually. I jerked at the rough familiarity.

"Get yourself over my lap, Stephanie. It's time for your first spanking."

I stared at him. Spanking? I hadn't had one of those since I was seven. I was sure his idea of a spanking was different from my father's.

"Stephanie, move your ass." Ethan dealt another, harder slap.

I said something rude about domineering men. He cut that off with a series of rough smacks.

I took the warning and scrambled to drape myself over him. He tugged me a bit until I was settled to suit him.

I could smell his leathers even better from here. They

were old and well-worn, rich with the aroma of years of polishing. I could feel the hard ridge under his zipper as it nudged my waist. I closed my eyes, trying not to think about its potential.

Ethan's big, rough hands ran over my naked rear end. I soon realized just how well those chaps framed me as he squeezed and fondled every inch of me. I liked the contact, the intimacy of his hands using me as he pleased, the contrast between my soft skin and his calluses.

The first blow caught me by surprise. It fell hard enough to get my attention but not as strong as what he'd dealt before. I swallowed, wondering what he intended.

"I want to see you good and red, Stephanie. Hot enough to melt ice and conscious of any touch."

He dealt a few more slaps in a slow, steady rhythm before stopping to fondle me. I sighed as he rubbed me, working the warmth across my skin.

"And, of course, I'll just keep going as long as I want," he whispered.

The spanking stayed slow for a while, until every part of my butt had felt the strength of his hand. Then he started to speed up, smacking me more strongly. I yelped and twisted but always followed his touch. He paused occasionally to fondle me, stroking my folds to encourage the wetness there. He spanked me harder still, between handling me and then probing me with his fingers.

I gasped at the first intrusion and thrust myself against him. Soon I was circling my hips and bucking up at him, whether for spanks or fondling.

Then he stopped. I panted and bit back a curse as I tried to regain control.

"On your knees, Stephanie," Ethan said quietly as he pushed me down between his legs.

I gathered myself together into the position he wanted, trying to ignore my unwilling excitement, and found the fly of his trousers in front of my eyes. I was fiercely glad at how much it bulged.

"Take it."

I promptly unzipped his leathers carefully and sighed at his readiness. Ethan's cock was beautiful, especially when it jutted eagerly. I traced a finger from the tiny slit at the top, over the head and down the beautiful branched vein on the thick shaft.

"Balls first."

I took a deep breath. We both knew that I loved going down on him. But this command meant that he wanted a long sensual pleasuring, not a quick rush to the finish. I had to set aside my body's demands for completion in order to obey him.

Ethan's balls were truly awesome, fat and low-hung behind their curtain of golden fur, when I lifted them gently out of the black leather. I nuzzled them, reacquainting myself with their musk, and then started to lick them. I caressed them with my tongue and cherished them with my mouth until they were hot and wet and tight.

"Now my cock." Ethan's voice was a little hoarse. I smiled privately and took one long, dragging lick up that beautiful vein. My tongue flickered against the sensitive point underneath the head and he groaned, sliding his hands into my hair. I smirked and began to explore, sweeping my tongue over him as I tried to work more and more of him into my mouth. I didn't manage to deep-throat him but the combination of my mouth and hands made a damn good impression on him.

"Pleasure yourself."

I blinked and put my hand down between my legs. My body quickly remembered its urgency and I started rocking between my hand and his cock. I twisted and writhed, self-control falling into shreds.

Ethan's hand clamped down over my arm, stopping its compulsive movements into me.

"Slower."

I whimpered but obeyed.

When I thought I couldn't bear it anymore, his hips started to hammer into my face. I opened my mouth further to take him and he poured his cream down my throat.

"Finish yourself." Ethan's voice was rough and deep but very emphatic. His hand lifted off my arm. I happily screwed my fingers deep into myself and rubbed my clit with the other hand. My climax came quickly, while I still had some of his essence in my mouth.

I crumpled onto the floor between his boots, panting for breath.

Ethan lifted me effortlessly up and onto the bed, laying me facedown. I closed my eyes and tried to recover.

The bed dipped under his weight as he sat down next to me. I started to roll over but he stopped me with a hand on my back.

"Lie still, Stephanie."

I relaxed again, more than willing not to exert myself yet.

His finger circled my asshole and I shivered at the familiar caress. He broke contact but soon returned, his finger greasy and slick. I twisted my head to see what he was doing. Ethan lifted an eyebrow at me.

"What the hell?"

"Did you think I'd stay out of your sweet ass forever?"

"Oh, no, you don't," I spluttered and tried to roll over. His hand pressed down harder, forcing me into the worn bedspread until I couldn't move.

I cursed him.

"What's the matter, Stephanie? Scared of some anal

sex?" he purred. "Think it'll hurt a tough cop like you? Or are you afraid that you'll like it too much?"

I let loose a string of words that I'd learned from drug pushers.

Ethan slapped my ass hard, reawakening the agony there. I shrieked.

"Lie still, Stephanie. Or else I really will make it difficult for you." His voice's cold implacable tones cut through my panic. I lay still and waited.

He stroked my asshole again and I quivered. Dammit, he knew I enjoyed being teased there, even if I'd never let more than a fingertip inside. He fondled me again and set his other hand to work through my folds.

I whimpered and hid my face in my arms. The bastard was going to make sure that I enjoyed this.

He slipped the first bead into my ass when I was focused solely on the fingers circling so casually around my clit.

I jerked but relaxed again, only to sob as a second bead entered me. The fullness surprised me and I tried to wriggle away. His other hand caught me roughly in exactly the stroke that always sends me over the edge. That climax kept me from noticing when the third bead came in.

Orgasms opened the way for the fourth and fifth beads as well, every bead larger than the one before.

I sprawled on the bed, convinced that my body was going to split in two, either from pleasure's aftershocks or the beads filling my backside. I knew exactly where each one was and its size. My body burned from their pressure.

"Time to go, Stephanie."

I opened my eyes and looked up at Ethan. He was immaculate again, his leathers showing no sign of excitement, past or present. His calm annoyed me. Then I thought about what he'd said.

"Ethan, dammit, what do you mean, go?"

"Move it, Stephanie," was all he said in response. I took a deep breath and sat up carefully, recognizing the inevitability of obedience. I may be stubborn but I'm not stupid.

The beads shifted inside me with the movement and I froze. I stood up tentatively, achingly conscious of the pressure inside with every movement.

Ethan held the leather jacket for me to put on and I carefully slid first one arm then the next inside. His leathers really did look untouched from this angle. My thighs stuck together slightly and I realized what I must look like.

"Ethan, can I please clean up first?"

"No."

"But, my chaps must be wet from my, uh . . ." I

fumbled for words under his eyes. I automatically finished buttoning the jacket.

"So what? You smell like sex, the best scent for a
woman."

"What?"

Ethan leaned down and kissed me. His hand slipped
under the jacket and between my legs. I jumped in surprise when he slid his fingers inside me but quickly
opened both my mouth and pussy to him. When he
lifted his head, I sagged against him like the worn-out
mattress on the bed behind us.

"Ohmygawd," I muttered, finally starting to understand what a sexual plaything felt like.

Ethan's mouth twitched.

He took me out of the room quickly, setting the
beads' silken tail with its ending ring to brush against my
legs. The beads rolled against each other, setting ripples
through my body and starting to make me welcome them.

"Ohmygawd," I said again when we stood in front
of his conveyance. Of course, he had brought his big
Harley motorcycle. It was new and faster than anything
the police had for enforcing speed limits. I really hoped
that nobody I knew would see us.

"Get on."

I sighed, resigned to my fate, and took a quick glance
around the parking lot for onlookers.

"Stephanie." Ethan's voice cracked like a whip and I flinched. "When I tell you to do something, just do it. I'll deal with any bystanders. If I want someone to watch, they'll do so."

"Dammit, Ethan," I protested.

His hand lifted my chin so that I had to face him.

"I like showing off my woman sometimes," he said evenly. "She had better enjoy it or she won't be kept around."

I bit my tongue against another useless objection.

"Good girl," he praised me and picked me up. I squeaked as he settled me onto the passenger's seat. My butt touched the cool leather and promptly remembered just how long and hard that spanking had been. I wriggled a little, trying to get comfortable. The beads' tail and ring caught between the seat and my legs, setting a corresponding tug through the beads and up my body. I tried to decide which was worse, my butt wanting to move around or the beads playing me with every twitch.

He straddled the bike and started it quickly, then handed me a helmet. I was holding it over my head when he spoke again.

"Just remember that I'm a vampire. The onlookers won't remember anything if I don't want them to."

My jaw dropped open. I believed him, all right, but what the hell did he have in mind?

He pulled on his own helmet, making him look like a futuristic knight and effectively ending the conversation. I quickly donned mine and wrapped my arms around him.

We hadn't gone two blocks before I realized that the big engine between my legs was torture, pure and simple. Its vibrations sent answering waves through the beads crammed into me. Echoes racked my body, clamoring for more sexual attention.

My orgasm flowered slowly just before we stopped.

By then, my head was buried between Ethan's shoulder blades. I couldn't think straight because everything I had was focused on the delicious sensations between my legs.

Ethan efficiently lifted the helmet off my head and strapped it onto the bike.

I straightened up slowly and looked around. We were at the outer edge of a parking lot filled with other motorcycles. I blinked and looked toward the building beyond the bikes. Its neon sign said simply "Frank's."

I closed my eyes and cursed. I'd only been here once before, a disturbance of the peace that ended in almost thirty arrests. Cops didn't come here without reinforcements, lots of them. If anyone here knew that I was a cop, I'd be in big trouble.

I let the thought trail away. I had to trust Ethan.

I slowly dismounted, moving as cautiously as an old woman with arthritis. My legs had more strength than I expected and I came upright with some semblance of normalcy.

"Come on."

I started toward the building, the beads' silken tail whispering against the leather. I tried very hard not to think about the beads' movements inside me or the way that my body was more than willing to climax again.

Just how many climaxes could one woman have during an evening, anyway? I was starting to be really afraid that Ethan was going to teach me the answer.

Ethan rubbed my butt idly and I stopped. He continued petting me and I shivered. Then I started walking again.

We went in quietly and I blinked at the mixture of loud noise and minimal lighting. The only real lights hung above each pool table, making the room a mixture of dark shadows and well-lit stages as men moved around, setting up their shots or chatting to their friends over a drink.

Ethan headed straight for the bar, keeping his arm around me. I matched his stride, biting my lip as my body's demand for another orgasm kept building. I wasn't listening when he spoke to the bartender. I came back to awareness again when he left the bar, holding a bottle in his left hand and his right still firmly against me.

A few steps saw us through a simple door and down a narrow passage. Another door led to a flight of steep stairs. I gasped when the first step sent my muscles clenching the damn beads in an entirely new and unforgettable fashion.

"Thinking about a fuck, Stephanie?"

Too far gone for words, I simply nodded and held on to the rail.

Ethan chuckled and picked me up, tossing me over his shoulder easily. He patted my ass lightly under the jacket and I swallowed at the sensation. Even the simplest contact now got me excited.

I closed my eyes to avoid dizziness as Ethan ran up the stairs. He sat me down on a table and I tried to catch my breath, gripping the table edge like a life vest. When he started to unbutton my jacket, I put my hands over his.

"Ethan," I whispered.

He kissed my hands.

"Hush, Stephanie, and look around."

I looked around slowly, prepared for the worst. We were alone in a small private dining room. I started to relax until a wave of sound hit me.

The private dining room was really just a balcony overlooking the pool hall. Its high railing hid people seated at the tables but allowed anyone standing to see everything happening below. I was on a table against that railing.

"Now take the jacket off and lie down on your stomach."

"But," I started to protest again.

"Just do it, Stephanie. They can't see you on the table. They can only hear you if you get loud."

I took a deep breath and got the jacket off as quickly as possible. Then I lay facedown on the long table, thankful that I'm usually a very quiet lover. It was covered with several layers of tablecloths, making it reasonably comfortable and clean.

I shivered slightly when a breeze from the ceiling fan crossed me. But Ethan's hands started to rub my back and I sighed, settling down to wait.

"A friend of mine taught me this way to enjoy an evening many years ago—1859, actually. He called it bourbon with a splash."

I yelped when a trickle of liquid ran down my spine, followed by Ethan's hot tongue.

"What the hell?"

"Bourbon, my dear."

I twisted my head to see him. His eyes were very green, dancing with mischief as he watched me.

"I'm going to drink this bottle of bourbon from your body." He swirled his finger through the traces still beading on my shoulder.

"Ohmygawd," was all I could think of to say.

He took a very long time drinking that bourbon. Every inch of bare skin on my back was anointed with bourbon and then savored with his tongue. He used his teeth too, nipping and scraping me until I was acutely sensitive to the lightest touch. He poured bourbon into the small of my back and then lapped it up like a cat. I shivered and writhed under him, moaning whenever his mouth found a particularly delicious point.

A thin trickle of bourbon found its way between my buttocks. I gasped and bucked at the totally unexpected intrusion. He spread me open and licked it away leisurely. He anointed me with more bourbon and stroked my folds while he enjoyed my taste. His fingers drove me frantic and I began to beg.

Ethan's mouth found my folds for the first time. I shrieked, totally heedless of any listeners, and climaxed.

Ethan rolled me onto my back and I slumped across the table, too spent for thought. He stroked my breasts, circling and fondling them until they knew more pleasure was waiting. My nipples hardened and ripened under his touch, begging for more attention. Then he bent his golden head and suckled me, so I sobbed and writhed under him. He twisted and bit my nipples roughly, which somehow made me even more excited.

When I was completely sensitized and eager for his touch again, he began to drink more bourbon from my body. This time he didn't permit any orgasms, no matter how much I begged. By the time he stopped, I would have willingly fucked every man in the building just to get satisfaction.

He stood over me and slowly unzipped his leather jeans. I watched greedily as he lifted himself out, his cock gleaming like a ruby in the dim light.

"Do you want this?"

"Damn you, yes," I hissed and reached for it. He slapped my hand away lightly and stepped back. I whimpered at the loss and looked at his face.

Ethan grasped my legs and pulled me down the table until I was barely braced on the end. He lifted my legs and spread them, opening me wide. I shuddered when my aching folds rubbed against his cock. I happily draped my legs over his shoulders, eager to be taken by him.

He entered me with a single quick thrust that left him buried to the hilt. He watched me adjust to the intense fullness within, from his big cock and the damn beads. Then he started to piston in and out of me, every movement deliberately rubbing against the beads through the thin but agonizingly sensitive membrane that separated them. I writhed and sobbed, my arousal building with every moment that saw me unfulfilled.

Then a single blunt finger rubbed my clit. I wailed as the first climactic pulse hit me. I shouted when he yanked the beads out of me fiercely, shooting me into a full-body orgasm. I didn't care how much noise we made; I was too damn glad.

I was barely aware when he climaxed.

I drifted for some time until I felt something sliding into my behind.

"Ethan?" I mumbled.

"Relax, Stephanie. I'm almost done."

I woke up more when I realized that he'd filled my asshole with something bigger and stiffer than the beads. I didn't want to fight any more of Ethan's ideas though.

"What did you do to me?" I murmured.

"There's a butt plug up your ass and a dildo in your cunt."

My eyes snapped open at his matter-of-fact response. I wriggled my hips slightly and my muscles clenched in response, tightening around two large, thick shafts. He really had stuffed me.

I gulped, feeling my body ache as it tried to adapt.

Ethan quickly anchored the two shafts to a leather strap passed between my legs and outside the chaps. He fastened that to a leather belt.

A jolt of pure hunger ran through me when I realized that I was locked up, available only to him.

"Now sit up and put your jacket on."

I obeyed Ethan quietly, more aware of the pressure within me than my undressed condition.

"Wait!" he snapped and I froze, leaving the jacket unbuttoned.

He bent his head to my mouth and I kissed him back, willingly yielding to him. His kiss was deep and hit me like a drug. When he lifted his head, I braced my hands behind me for support, arching my breasts toward him unconsciously.

"Very nice," he murmured and suckled me. I enjoyed his attentions shamelessly, twisting under him to make sure that both breasts received equal attention. He chuckled and attended me until my nipples became hard buds. I was as eager for sex as if I hadn't had a man in months.

He stopped and I saw a flashing bit of metal in his hand. It caught my nipple a moment later and I gasped at the unaccustomed pain. It didn't hurt too much though and soon turned into a dull ache. Then another clamp bit down on my other breast.

I swore softly but accepted them, seeing my nipples turn red as berries beyond them.

"Good girl," Ethan murmured and I flushed at the rare praise. He buttoned the jacket quickly so that my engorged nipples pressed against its silk lining. Then he lifted me onto my feet.

"You're going to walk out of here now, Stephanie. I want to watch you as those shafts fill you and the jacket rubs you."

My eyes widened. I could feel the first aches starting where he had mentioned. I nodded in response.

"Now, Stephanie."

I walked to the door slowly, acutely aware of every shift and tremble within me. The silk rasped my breasts until I almost forgot the clamps' pain.

Ethan took his time getting us outside. I wanted to scream at him to hurry so we could get away from the knowing eyes that never looked at us directly. I also wanted to go more slowly so I would have a better chance of regaining my poise after every pulse that the two shafts sent through me.

I didn't think about the effect the motorcycle would have on me until we stood in front of it. When I realized that, I cursed its ancestry in terms that would have gotten me thrown out of any football or baseball game.

Ethan lifted me onto the motorcycle and handed me the helmet. He didn't speak, although his eyes were bright with amusement and hunger.

Awareness seeped through me as I considered the future. Then I smiled back at him, confident of his need for me. I knew he would feed from me.

We rode out on the Harley at a brisk pace, faster than I would have taken that narrow road. But I trusted Ethan's vampire reflexes and gave myself up to enjoyment. The dildo and butt plugs throbbed inside me, like the pleasure to come. My nipples ached in a constant reminder of his attentions.

I tightened my arms around Ethan and rubbed myself deliberately against his back. His hard strength made my breasts hurt more, reminding me of previous encounters when he had suckled them until they bled. We jolted across a bump and the first climax rocked me.

Ethan glanced back over his shoulder at me but I couldn't see his expression through the helmet's visor. I rubbed myself against him again. His hand squeezed my knee and I closed my eyes at the caress.

We paused once at a railroad crossing. I dropped my hands down into his lap and played with him.

Unfortunately, the train was gone before I could unzip his leathers.

I was lost in my own world of wind and lust when the motorcycle stopped, my body soft and sated. I smiled at Ethan when he took my helmet off.

"You reek of bourbon and sex, woman."

"Yes, sir," I agreed. It was obviously wise to agree with Ethan, especially when he spoke the truth.

"A night in the drunk tank is definitely called for."

"What?"

My brain clicked back into action with a rush and I looked around quickly. We were parked behind San Leandro's police station with no other vehicles around. It was a small station, suitable for a rural town that only needed one cop on night duty.

I stared up at Ethan, trying to understand.

"You ever fantasized about being a prisoner? Ever wanted to be locked up and used until your body faded from pleasure?"

I nodded slowly.

"Then stand up, prisoner, so we can carry out your sentence."

I dismounted to stand on legs shaky from past pleasures and fear of the immediate future.

Ethan quickly cuffed my hands, linking them to a

belt, before he shackled my feet. I shuffled experimentally, recognizing the chains as those used for transporting prisoners. A little voice inside me shouted in anticipation, as I understood my helplessness. It felt so damn good to be purely feminine and not have to worry about being in control.

Ethan led me into the police station. I hesitated when I saw the camera above the door.

"Relax, Stephanie. It's not working tonight. I don't want a record of this either."

I nodded and shuffled after him down the hallway, finding no other cameras around.

"Face the wall, prisoner."

I obeyed quickly. Ethan kicked my feet apart expertly, then ran his hands over me harshly and efficiently.

I trembled at the touch, so familiar from my own past actions but so different when done by my lover.

He unbuttoned the jacket and slid it down my shoulders. Then he stroked my breasts, plumping them in his hands and running his fingers out towards the tips. I leaned back against him in a haze of sensation.

He turned me to face him and smoothly plucked the clamps off one at a time. I groaned as pain rushed into my nipples. Ethan licked and sucked my breasts, combining pleasure with agony until I ached.

"Please," I whispered, unsure of what I wanted.

Ethan guided me into the jail cell, an old-fashioned one with a barred door. I dropped to my knees at his rough command and leaned over the cot. Shamelessly, eagerly, I circled my hips in invitation. The only thing that mattered to me now was getting him inside me.

I felt his heat when he knelt behind me. He rubbed himself against me and I moaned at the feel of the smooth leather that separated me from him. The belt fell away and his hand ran down my belly, finding and jostling the dildo in my cunt.

I couldn't think, couldn't breathe. My need for him was a deeper agony than what crowned my breasts.

"Now comes the splash, Stephanie, when my cream spills out of your backside."

He twisted the plug, screwing it into my backside. I gripped it with deep unfamiliar muscles, welcoming the connection with him.

He growled when my seeking hips rubbed against his hand. My need surged and shouted at his response. He yanked the plug free and I gasped at the sudden emptiness.

Then I felt the blunt tip of his cock press against my ass. I pushed back to welcome it and felt it slip in. I froze in panic at its size, fatter than anything I had accepted before. Then I remembered the satisfaction he had given me earlier. My muscles remembered how he had trained them to spread at his touch.

He kept still until my body softened and opened for him. Then he slid into me on a slow, steady wave.

I burned, but the pain of stretching quickly became a delicious agony of fullness. I braced my hands on the cot underneath me. Then he began to move.

He rode me with an intensity that demanded everything of me. I enjoyed it like nothing I had ever felt before. I was his woman to use as he chose. His raw hunger spurred me into an answering frenzy. Our grunts and snarls sounded primitive and entirely suitable for that harsh room.

I tried hard not to come before he did. I wanted to feel every slightest pulse of him deep inside me.

Ethan didn't permit that, of course. He leaned over my back like a wolf and nuzzled my neck. He licked and sucked at the pulse there until I twisted under him, forgetting everything else. He bit down hard and fast so that blood erupted between us, catapulting me into an orgasm that took over my entire body.

I felt his hot cream burst inside me.

I woke up the next morning back in my shabby motel room. I don't know when he brought me back but I do remember that he had me more than once in that little cell.

My wrists and ankles were only slightly sore from the cuffs and shackles. The bite marks on my neck took longer to heal than usual but they're gone now.

I trust him more than I did before, which is an odd thing to say about a vampire. We have an understanding of sorts that feels almost like need for each other. We never discussed any changes in our relationship and I don't plan to ask him. There'll be time enough to see what happens when we meet again.

In the meantime, I'm going to try drinking bourbon.

traffic stop

a tale of ethan templeton

Steve came back into the bedroom quietly and stood still for a moment, watching Ethan sleep. He was asleep, not dead, no matter what he looked like or how cold his body felt. She'd seen him wake up more than once at sunset, coming fully conscious as the last daylight faded beyond the horizon.

Her lover. Her partner too, at least while that murderer was still out there.

She took off her gun and set it on the nightstand. Ethan would protect her better than it ever could. Strange thing for a Texas Ranger to say about a vampire.

Steve sat down on the chair and began to take off her boots, wondering how she'd come to trust him so much. Her subconscious promptly unrolled the memory for her. She'd remembered it so often, especially on the long waits that defined a cop's life. Now it unrolled before her as she'd once told her girlfriends.

✦

J met the sexiest guy while I was working out in the Hill Country. It was a little town but they had big ideas about their cops. Wanted us to be a real spit-shined bunch, no matter what we were doing. A good place to start out, especially if you'd always wanted to be a cop.

I got off late that night. I didn't have a date so I headed home on the scenic route. Not many guys want to date a girl with a third-degree black belt in karate, rated expert in pistol and rifle, who can bench press over 150 pounds.

It was clear that night with a full moon so I could see a long ways ahead as I drove. Coming down one hill, I saw a late-model black pickup speeding in front of me. He was going at least ninety so I did my duty. It took almost five miles of flashing lights before I got him to stop. I was pretty steamed by that long of a chase but I calmed down some while I ran his plates. They came back clear and I headed out to talk to him.

He had rolled down the window and looked at me when I came up. My heart stopped beating. Anglo, sandy hair, and hazel eyes. Just a gorgeous hunk of bad boy. Yum . . .

As soon as I saw him, all I wanted to do was haul him out of the cab and jump his bones. His eyes had a look in them that said "Sex!" and I wanted lots with him. I tried to cool down and talk to him about speed limits though.

He just sat there and nodded, gave me his license when I asked for it, and looked at me. I kept getting hotter and hotter thinking about all the things I could be doing with a man who watched me the way he did.

I took his license back to my cruiser and ran it through the system, trying to cool down. The license came back clean and I got out, only to find him standing next to the door watching me. Six feet, one hundred eighty pounds of pure muscle perfect for giving a girl a good time.

Well, I did what any self-respecting female cop would do: I told him we needed to talk, and I needed to search him. Then I told him to put his hands on the hood. He gave me one steady look that saw every detail of my uniform. He even checked to see how much chest I have under my Kevlar vest. Then he turned around and put his hands down flat. His beautiful butt was pushed out toward me, just begging for appreciation. I could see the muscles under that thin white Western shirt, hard muscles echoed in the strong legs below.

I ran my flashlight down his back, following that smooth flow of muscle. He pushed his hips back some, letting me know that he liked the touch. I teased his waistband with the flashlight but couldn't get inside. So I told him to take off the belt. He dropped the belt next to him and went back to standing there, watching me over his shoulder with a half-smile in the moonlight. Mostly he kept his mouth closed when he smiled but I thought I saw some pretty sharp teeth there for a moment.

My hand slowly slid down inside his jeans over that beautiful butt. I did a full cavity search of that man. All I found was the best set of masculine jewels that you're ever going to find. And I searched carefully and thoroughly . . .

When I was done, he was standing there with his jeans on the road next to his feet. Somehow his boots had gotten tossed off to one side. One of them didn't look quite right; maybe he had a knife in it. But I didn't care about that. I was much more interested in that big thick dick rearing up to greet me, looking more than ready for a long night's ride.

The radio blared something. I answered it with some

garbage, anything to keep that old biddy Louise in Dispatch from bothering me for the rest of the night.

He hadn't moved when I came back to him, just kept on looking like sex on the hoof leaning against my cruiser. I turned off my flashlight after another good long perusal. I fumbled putting it back onto my belt and my hands touched the cuffs hanging there.

A moment later, I had him facing the cruiser again, hands cuffed behind his back, and was feeling a bit more in control. His head twisted around to see me but he stayed calm. His eyes did get a little greener in the moonlight and his smile a little wider with those silver bracelets around his wrists though.

I put a hand on his shoulder and turned him around while I thought about what to do next. You'd think that I'd just jump him but I didn't. I told him to take my clothes off. His eyes really gleamed at that order and he bowed to me just a bit. Looked rather like a tiger whose animal trainer had just cracked the whip.

Well, he took my entire uniform off, one piece at a time. First my belt yielded to his mouth's persuasion, then my trousers, then my . . .

He had the strongest teeth and tongue too; didn't have any real problem getting even that Kevlar vest off me. He just kept working at the uniform, and items kept sliding off me. Of course, he got in lots of little licks and bites at the same time. A mouth like that didn't need the help of hands to get a girl worked up and undressed. I was hot and shaking, almost moaning by the time he finished.

Then I sat down on the hood and spread my legs wide. He didn't need any more invitation than that. Just went straight down on his knees and applied his mouth to where it would do the most good. I threw my head back and rode his face, my legs gripping his head like it was the finest bronc in Texas. I jumped when he nipped me and felt the blood running down my leg. But mostly it just felt so damn good that I kept ordering him to give me more.

He started working his way up my body and I started grabbing at him to bring him closer. His mouth fastened on mine and I opened up to him like a 9mm Beretta welcoming a magazine of ammunition. My arms and legs wrapped around him and we fell back on the hood together, one sweaty, heaving mass of flesh. He thrust home, I threw my head back and he bit me on the neck.

I was really glad then for the sergeant's insistence on having a good-looking cruiser. All those wax jobs that I'd cursed at sure came in handy when a bad boy is pumping your body across the hood. . . .

I woke up the next morning, naked as a jaybird in the backseat of my cruiser. I had bruises all over me, plus scratches and bites. It looked like I'd gone five rounds with the champion and the ache between my legs confirmed his prowess. I pulled my uniform on and headed home for a quick shower and change before going on duty again.

The worst bite, on my neck over my jugular, healed within two days so no one at the station ever noticed anything.

The hardest part to explain was why my handcuffs had to be replaced. I'd found them in pieces next to the cruiser and, well, I couldn't tell the sergeant what had been going on before that bad boy snapped them, could I?

And I thanked my guardian angel that I never had to discuss this night with my sergeant. He'd have fired me for sure if he knew just what went on that night. . . .

✦

Steve sat still, watching Ethan sleep. Her neck itched and she rubbed it reflexively.

Her finger came away with a drop of blood.

Ethan's chest slowly rose. And fell.

She smiled, the contented smirk of a tabby cat eyeing a fresh saucer of milk as the sky darkened outside.

apex predator

a tale of don rafael perez
with mention of ethan templeton

April 5 (Davis, California)

Dreamed again last night of Rodrigo, my medieval Spanish knight. He was dressed in full armor, with a chain mail coif draping his head. The dream was remarkably vivid: I could hear him singing a cantiga about a knight who had unwillingly left his beloved to follow the king's orders. His gaze was soft and a little absent-minded, as he hummed more than sang the melancholy lyrics.

May 31 (and my first chance to write
in my diary since I moved here)

San Leandro, Texas: It's a very small town (five hundred
people at most) and I've got a little house on the out-
skirts with an acre of land. It's the most space I've had in
my life, except when doing fieldwork. My old pickup
fits in just fine, as do my T-shirts, jeans, and boots. It's
only twenty minutes to the rescue center and I've been
working there for a week now.

I'm damn lucky to have the job at the raptor center
here. Not many good jobs for wildlife veterinarians
around, let alone one that combines research and veteri-
nary medicine with owls. The center's staff has been
very friendly and even put in a rush order for the name
tag on my office door: *Grania O'Malley, M.S., D.V.M.,*
Ph.D. How cool was that? They even hugged me when I
cried over seeing my name for the first time with all
those degrees I'd worked for years to get.

Wonder what the available guys are like down here,
an hour out of Austin?

June 1 (afternoon)

Today I took part in the monthly open house at the raptor center, where I gave a few tours. In between walking

people around, I wound up back in the big library/conference room where the refreshments were laid out.

Late in the afternoon after the crowd thinned out, I made conversation with Caleb Jones, a geologist working for Santiago Oil & Gas. Surprisingly, he was wearing a Kevlar vest under his starched cowboy shirt. (Wonder if Santiago Oil & Gas is a subsidiary of the enigmatic Santiago Trust? When I researched the center and this neighborhood, I heard rumors that the trust was older than Texas, richer than Fort Knox, harder to figure out than the Pentagon, and more dangerous to its enemies than a nuclear bomb.)

As we sipped watery lemonade, Caleb and I chatted about our scientific specialties, the local ecosystem, professors we'd suffered under, and other standard academic social topics, while waiting for his boss. Caleb's a very nice guy but not available for dating. At least not with women, since he was definitely very aware of every good-looking male that passed by.

Then a big cowboy walked in the other end of the library, gliding like the mountain lion I saw once in Utah. My mouth went dry. He could have been my knight's twin.

He had raven-black hair, as thick and glossy as in my dreams, which reached to the bottom of his collar. A memorable face with olive skin and a light shadow of beard, not pretty but so very strong. His nose was as aquiline as an eagle's beak, and that mobile mouth looked capable of both singing poetry and shouting battle orders. He stood just under two meters tall—or six feet-five—all of it heavily muscled, as if he could fight in armor against Saracens all day and all night. He strolled past the bookshelves with the slightly rolling gait of a man who spends more time in the saddle than on his feet.

His face was surprisingly young—about my age— even with the slashing scar on his forehead. But I grieved to see that his eyes were ancient and guarded, despite the polite social smile he wore. He exuded competence and the quiet aura of danger, a man who didn't give a damn what the world thought of him because he could remake it to suit himself.

I was so stunned, my knees almost gave out under me. I've never understood girls who had one-night stands with strangers but I'd have had one there and then with that big cowboy, no matter who was watching.

He walked straight up to Caleb, who introduced him to me as his boss, Rafael Perez. I automatically held out my hand and he kissed it.

When the hell had anything like that ever happened to me? I gulped and tried to think of something polite to say other than "How about a fuck, cowboy?" I did manage to stammer "Señor Perez" like an adolescent schoolgirl.

He said something polite about my working at the center that didn't require much of an answer, then excused Caleb and himself. And my heartbeat finally had a chance to return to normal.

Still behaving like a schoolgirl, I drifted over to the window to see them leave. Two identical big new Mercedes sedans waited for them, not pickups or SUVs; classy and expensive, to match those well-worn Lucchese alligator boots he was wearing.

But his party—entourage, really—made me stare. Five men, all with the thick chests denoting Kevlar vests hidden under their cowboy shirts, were lounging beside the cars. As deceptively innocent as a pride of lions by a watering hole—and as ready to spring into action. I'd have bet a month's rent they could have stopped an armed attack in a matter of seconds, without turning a hair.

They came to attention as I watched and quickly pulled one big sedan up to the center's entrance. Rafael got into the back seat and Caleb took the wheel, while the previous driver—a particularly deadly looking fellow—slid over to ride shotgun. As the two cars turned down the long driveway to the highway, both vehicles displayed the slightly too solid handling of armored vehicles.

Why on earth would an oil industry executive be protected so heavily? Were the rumors about the Santiago Trust true? A chill ran down my spine.

June 1 (evening)

I couldn't relax after that, of course, even with the next two days off. So I decided to do some owling, my favorite way to unwind. I do so love to see and hear owls.

After changing clothes, I went out with my night–vision goggles and camera. I studied the map and then drove the center's boundaries. It's completely within a public park whose big lake was very busy, even allowing for the Memorial Day holiday week.

The center itself is toward one edge of the park, which borders some private land. (Wonder if the owners are yet another Santiago Trust subsidiary?) It's rough terrain so it's never been farmed or ranched; the ecosystem is still virgin. Bob, the center's director, wants to do research there. The owners haven't said yes, but haven't said no either. He's hoping to coax them into agreeing.

The evening was a joy, with more owls than I'd hoped for. It's the events after that that baffle me. But

I'm just going to record all the facts, at least the ones that can be documented. I can analyze them later, after time gives me some perspective. There's got to be a good scientific theory to cover this, if I can just come up with it.

I gradually worked my way toward the lake. It was fairly quiet by then since most of the people had gone to bed. I could see a lightning storm light up the sky miles away but it was miserably hot and humid where I was. The mesquite smell was quite distinct and I tried not to get too many twigs caught in my hair.

I finally settled just within a thicket, watching a really magnificent horned owl. I slowed my breathing, using some yoga exercises, and let myself blend into the scene. After a while, I could hear the small animals start moving around as they became accustomed to my presence.

I heard two people coming. Actually I heard the woman first. She was loud, with a voice that combined the worst of Brooklyn and Texas. The man kept kissing her, which shut her up some. But then he'd do something else that freed up her mouth and she'd start letting loose with that voice. She had a filthy mouth, talking about what she wanted from him. It sounded as if he was carrying through on her requests, too.

I stayed where I was since I didn't have an easy way to get out of there unnoticed. Okay, I was curious too.

When I'm married, I want to be a good lover but how can I learn? I could count all my past lovers on the fingers of one hand and still have digits left over. Real-life examples would be much more useful than adult videos; I've always wondered just how real the wall-to-wall-sex DVDs were that'd been passed around the dorms a few hundred times.

They stopped in the clearing next to my thicket and I could see them easily, thanks to those military prototype night-vision goggles Bob had so kindly loaned me.

The woman was blonde, with breasts that came from a catalog, not genetics. Very fit, fashionably dressed.

The man was big, two meters tall, muscular, black hair, and dark eyes—strong profile; I'll remember that face forever.

It was Rafael Perez.

I couldn't believe my eyes. What the hell was he doing making out in the woods with a woman? I'd have sworn he had money, certainly enough for a hotel room.

He kissed her and kneaded those breasts through her T-shirt. She wasn't wearing a bra and I immediately saw her breasts become firmer, the nipples more prominent. And damned if my breath didn't catch as an answering thrill ran through my body from my throat to my core. My nipples rubbed against my cheap white cotton bra, as if Rafael's hand was kneading them through the cloth too.

She moaned some and clutched at him, definitely enjoying herself. I fought to control my own breathing, as my pulse sped up. More than anything else, I did not want them to know I was watching, especially when my breasts were aching and liquid heat was building between my legs.

Pretty soon he had his hand up her skirt and she started humping his fingers ferociously. Every muscle in my body wanted to rock with her but I couldn't, wouldn't let myself do so. Yet the battle somehow made me more aware of the fire building inside me, more conscious of the strength of his arm. My hunger grew to see what his hand was doing so that my body could echo the effects.

He quickly pulled her T-shirt off. Then his hands really became busy, fondling her with more skill than I'd ever seen in an adult video. Mercifully, his mouth stayed over hers and kept her fairly quiet, except for grunts and such.

And oh, how I wanted those hands to be touching me. Kneading and smoothing my breasts, lifting and plucking my nipples, sweeping up from my core to my ribs and up to my agonizingly hard nipples. . . . She moaned her pleasure and her need. Her leg lifted and reached over his hip, opening her further to him. In my mind, I hissed at her to do more of that so I could see more of him.

I started to arch my back instinctively as if I, too, could lean into his caress. A strand of hair caught on a thorn and I froze, warned by the almost infinitesimal change in tension. I could not move, could not make a sound, could not change my breathing lest they know I was there. My core tightened in protest then focused more strongly on Rafael and his lover—and heated faster.

He eased her down on the ground, with her legs spread. I could see far too many details for my comfort—how flushed she was, how incredibly wet, how she rocked with increasing excitement. The skillful movements of his fingers playing through her folds.

My folds swelled, rubbing against my cotton panties, pouring cream. My clit was swollen, aching, as if Rafael was inciting me.

I tried to close my eyes but I had to look again. I tried to think of something else, tried to recite multiplication tables but gave up when I couldn't remember what four times five was. I tried to recite my dissertation, which I'd worked on for so many years that I'd memorized it. But now I couldn't get past the first paragraph.

His hand kept working her, masturbating her until she started coming in a series of waves. I'm sure she was having multiple orgasms.

I fought my body's demand to do the same.

Then his mouth left hers, setting her free to start screeching again, and he bit her on the neck. It wasn't a nice little nip either but a deep puncture.

I choked, shaken to the bone.

He stopped for just an instant while his eyes searched the clearing. I went as still as I could, trying to make myself invisible.

A little voice whispered in my head, "*Go away.*" I ignored the voice; I couldn't leave the thicket without making noise.

The small voice kept urging me to leave, but I stayed where I was. A headache built behind my eyes as the voice got louder, until it almost reached a shout. Still, I somehow managed not to panic and run but remained in the thicket.

He evidently didn't see me because his attention went back to her. He pulled her across him until I could see every inch of what happened to her and how she responded. Then he began to play with her again, his hands working her breasts as he crooned into her ears.

And my traitorous body, which obviously deeply resented being denied its orgasm, promptly started heating up again. In fact, it climbed faster than I'd have thought possible, especially when his hand delved between her legs. She was calling him her favorite stud as cream ran past her thighs. I shuddered to think of just how far down my pants I too was wet.

Her hips rocked hard against his hand when he shoved his third finger into her. He started to suck her and she was moaning happily as she started climbing for another orgasm. I could see his cheeks hollow as he drank her blood. She climaxed hard, screaming happily when he bit down.

And heaven help me, I climaxed at the same time she did. Without lifting a finger, without touching myself. Only from watching Rafael with his lover.

My brain began to work again.

He was still lapping gently at her when I opened my eyes again, so very little time had passed. He hadn't taken much though, probably a little less than a pint.

Functional fangs, apparently razor-sharp, comparable to those on a vampire bat. I shuddered. But those pests required their prey be asleep, not at an orgasmic climax.

The only other choice I could think of was that he was a vampire. But I can't believe that. Vampires are creatures of myth and legend, studied by social scientists. No veterinarian, or other trained biologist, has ever observed one.

I started wondering what I should do. Should I try to stop him? How?

But all the time, I could hear that screech of hers, carrying on like he was God's gift to women. So I continued to observe them, telling myself that I must be mistaken, that she wasn't being hurt. Besides, he looked so much like my knight, who would never, ever injure a woman—and wasn't that a most illogical thought?

She caressed his head when he stopped drinking. He began to lick her shoulder and she just kept petting him, talking about how good he was in little gasps. When she'd recovered herself and her voice was back to its usual volume, he helped her to get dressed. Very courteous behavior, just like my knight.

They walked back toward the lake together, arm in arm. After giving them a head start, I slipped out of the thicket and followed them cautiously, as quietly as I could.

Soon that Brooklyn blonde's mouth was working again, this time paying Rafael the most ridiculous compliments. "You're better than my chocolate truffles," she purred once and leaned up to kiss him.

I gritted my teeth.

They split up just before they reached the marina. She kissed him on the cheek and went on alone, singing a pop song.

He watched her go while I kept an eye on him from behind a big live oak, beside the road. I had the night-vision goggles off by then, given the extra light from the marina.

When she was out of sight, he stretched his arms and legs, then his back. He looked almost like a bird preening on its nest. He was graceful too, which is hard to believe of someone that muscular.

Suddenly he shimmered and I blinked in surprise. When I focused again, a very big horned owl was taking off from where the man had been standing. (I know that owl wasn't there before. I have no explanation for this yet; I'm just recording what I saw.)

I stepped out to investigate Rafael's disappearance. Suddenly a man's arm slammed around my neck and dragged me back against him, using a choke hold. I fought hard, using every dirty trick I'd ever learned, but to no avail. The fellow was simply much stronger than I was; he never even grunted when I kicked him. He wasn't Rafael, being only a few inches taller than myself and more slender than Rafael. At least he was professional enough not to have a hard-on. Finally I forced myself to relax, trying not to curse him or visibly seethe, and wait for an opportunity to escape.

Then Rafael walked onto the road, clad only in his shirt and jeans, and faced me. *"Buenas noches, doctora."*

What the hell was going on here? Where the hell had he been? Where were the rest of his clothes, like those Lucchese boots?

"Did you enjoy your observations, *doctora*?"

I could have killed him for that quip. After all, he was the one who'd been behaving outrageously by drinking blood. I forced myself to be calm again and wait for an opening. I'd talked my way past murderous thugs in Colombian swamps while counting owls and survived; surely I could deal with a pair of Texans.

The man behind me relaxed slightly but his grip on me was still implacable.

"Your activities were somewhat unusual, *señor*." That headache was after me again, just like in the woods.

"Do you intend to share them with others?"

"What's to share? A man and woman did some necking in the woods. Would anyone in authority believe the man bit the woman for a nefarious reason, especially when the man is such an important member of the community?"

"Do you mock me, *doctora*?" My captor's forearm tightened against my windpipe.

I swallowed, hard, and reminded myself they had power here, not me. Always be polite, as the sisters at the orphanage said. I modulated my tone to genuine meekness. "No, I'm just telling the truth."

He studied me then nodded. The forearm left my throat but my attacker didn't release me.

"How discreet are you, *doctora?*"

"If the lady is unharmed, I will be completely discreet." This at least was the truth. Besides, who'd believe me if I talked?

"So very much the medical practitioner. If I hear you have been indiscreet about tonight's activities, you will immediately regret it. Greatly."

"If I learn that the lady has been harmed in any way, you, sir, will immediately regret it. Greatly."

He smiled at my ferocity. "Upon my honor, I would never harm a lady." He bowed to me, as formally as if at the royal court in Madrid. Oddly enough, I believed him and relaxed slightly.

"*Con perdón*, may I remove this impertinent thorn from your shirt, *doctora?*"

What on earth did he really want? But his expression was completely sincere. My captor's grip on my arms loosened slightly, from bone-crushing to firm.

I eyed him suspiciously, the only sound waves lapping gently against the shore, before agreeing.

"You may depart, Ethan."

Ethan hesitated. If anything, his grip tightened on me. "She could be the bait for another assassination attempt, Don Rafael."

Assassination???

"There is no threat to me here and now." Rafael's voice was deadly calm—and it sliced the night air like my best scalpel.

"As you wish, sir." My jailer reluctantly released me and was gone—without a sound.

Rafael then slowly plucked thorns and twigs and many other souvenirs of a long walk in the woods off me. I submitted, all too conscious of Rafael's big hands moving so carefully and almost respectfully over me. Something deep inside me, beyond my mind's control, whispered agreement and pleasure in his touch, as if he were the most welcome of lovers. My muscles slowly unclenched as my pulse slowed to a more normal beat. My eyes slowly drifted shut, the night's tensions starting to drift away, as he behaved like a gentleman.

"Will you exchange the kiss of peace with me, as a token of your pledge?" Rafael asked quietly, as he finished.

I agreed cautiously, expecting a polite peck on the cheek. I took a formal stance before him, my hands resting lightly on his shoulders in an old folk dance hold, and waited.

"Ah, *doctora*," he murmured and bent his head. He brushed his lips against my temple, gentle and undemanding. I relaxed and started to move away, hoping my contact with him was over.

Then he kissed me again, which was very different. It was a lover's kiss, mouth to mouth, starting slow, growing bolder and bolder as we enjoyed each other more and more. My body remembered how much it had enjoyed watching him with that blonde—and began to happily become aroused.

My hands slid down from his shoulders, over his arms, exploring the iron-heat of his biceps. I murmured my approval and tilted my head back to smile at him, everything in me seeming to slowly swirl into a lava pool of lust.

"Ah, *doctora*, your kisses are more heated than your hair," Rafael purred, stroking my back until I stretched against him like a cat begging for more. I rubbed my leg along the outside of his, the roughness of our jeans heating the fire in my core still further. I sighed and slid my hand into his hair, unconscionably eager for more kisses.

"*Querida*." He bent his head toward me again.

Just then headlights swept over us briefly, as a car twisted and turned along the lakeshore road, no more than two miles away. I sprang away from him, cursing, and our all-too-intimate moment ended. "*Buenas noches, Señor Perez.*"

"*Hasta luego, Doctora O'Malley.*" He lifted a hand to me and disappeared into the woods before I could challenge his assumption. See you later, indeed!

After that, I headed for the lake, where I spotted the woman as she was boarding a big houseboat. She moved easily with no sign of weakness or injury. I could see lights and hear voices from the boat's cabin so I didn't try to question her then.

Now what do I do? Tell the police? They wouldn't believe me; I'm not sure I believe myself.

The first thing to do is check to see if he injured her at all. If so, I'll try to talk her into seeing a doctor, maybe the cops. If not, then I'll keep quiet until I've got some observations worth reporting.

I wish I had some family to talk this over with. I'm proud of having made my own way in the world. But occasionally I wish I wasn't a foundling, the daughter of a dead drug kingpin and his heroin-addict girlfriend. At times like this, I long for a big family who'd support me, no matter what happened.

June 1 (later that night)

I was still thinking about what I'd observed while I got ready for bed. So I took a shower to relax, the water running gently down me from the big, old-fashioned shower head.

I kept seeing Rafael as he stood behind the blonde, his arms wrapped around her. She must have been able to feel every inch of him—his arms, chest, hips, legs, cock. But he'd never satisfied himself. Instead he'd bent every effort to pleasuring her. What had that felt like?

His breath stirring her hair, ruffling the strands like the water flowing down my neck. Making me so very aware of every sensitive nerve that a lover could map with his mouth or the delicate touch of his teeth, like the slightly heavier beat of the water.

The strength of his chest behind his shirt, curved against her back. Cloth and muscles as close to her and moving as smoothly and constantly against her as the water against my skin, warm as the shower. . . .

I think I moaned as I fondled my breasts, mimicking how he'd blatantly aroused hers. I know my hand slipped between my legs to play with myself. I was flushed, panting, hotter than the shower's temperature could explain.

I remembered the contrast between his shirt and his belt, snug against her hips. And the muscles moving under his jeans, when she had opened herself for him . . .

His fly must have been nestled against the seam in her backside. Like the water running down my back, finding that seam, gliding down the inside of my legs as if remembering the contrast between the masculinity of denim trousers and the femininity of a frilly skirt.

I spread my legs a little wider, one hand taking up the most familiar rhythm for getting off. But my other hand began to tease me, miming how a man's cock could test and encourage his lover. Flashes of heat lanced me, centered in my core. Breathing was becoming harder as my hips started to rock.

How his leg had slid between hers and spread her, how he'd suddenly thrust three fingers into her. . . .

I too thrust three fingers—and came, stretched wider than I've ever been for a lover, screaming his name, as my body exploded in a single, massive, ecstatic jolt, which slammed me against the wall.

Some time later, I woke up, when cold water started pouring from the showerhead. I've never lost consciousness before from an orgasm.

I'm going to bed now. The scientific analysis can wait until tomorrow.

June 2 (before dawn)

I can't believe the dream I just had. I'm writing it down now, while I still remember it. Hopefully it'll seem less important in the morning.

I dreamed that I was a horned owl, flying through the night skies with another owl. It was incredibly vivid;

I could feel the wind lifting my wings, its sound being muffled by my feathers. The larger owl and I seemed to be playing, gliding and dipping above the trees. It was more fun than anything I've ever imagined.

Just because I could, I swooped over a meadow to see the flowers. I alighted amid some bluebonnets and quickly turned back into myself, laughing quietly. The other owl landed behind me and a man wrapped his arms around me, chuckling.

I leaned back against him and realized that it was Rafael. Neither of us wore any clothing, which seemed very unimportant then, almost customary for us. I savored the feel of that big, strong body giving its heat to me. I could feel his chest move as he breathed in and out against my back. I could see his forearms resting against me, their black hairs silvered by the moon.

I felt safe. And happy and cherished.

I turned around in his arms and kissed him. A very gentle kiss, the lightest possible contact as I chortled. I could feel his mouth soften and move against mine in a sweet dance. Then his tongue delicately glided over my lips, in an elegant mimicry of the dance we'd shared in the skies above.

My hand slid up the back of his neck until my palm rested on the strong muscles and my fingers tangled in his hair. It was long, thick, and silky—and irresistible to me. My other hand soon joined it and I lost myself in his kiss as my mouth opened for him.

The only thing that existed then was his mouth, his hands holding me close, and his hard body against me. I lived for the connection with him.

When he lifted his head, we laughed together for joy. I have never laughed as much as I did in this dream.

That kiss proves that this was just a dream. Nobody can kiss like that, not that I've ever heard of or experienced. Perhaps in books but even there, only in fiction.

June 2

I started the day determined to come up with a theory to explain last night's events.

A web search returned too many hits to be quickly absorbed.

Interviewing the blonde told me that she was perfectly healthy and of sound mind but didn't tell me anything about vampires.

Austin's academic libraries had some information but no impartial, third-person accounts of vampires.

However, local bookstores did provide some useful information. (Note to self: Pick up more beans at the local market. I've just ruined the food budget yet again by buying books.) But these accounts raised more questions than they answered. The current literature, whether non-fiction or fiction, does not agree on what a vampire is or does. So I started describing vampires on my own.

Apex predator at the top of the food chain.

Feeds primarily or solely on blood.

Hunting technique emphasizes sexual attraction.

May or may not kill prey.

May or may not be seen in daylight.

May or may not be capable of sexual acts, specifically orgasm and/or ejaculation.

I tried to figure out the details of a vampire's attack, see if there were any vulnerabilities in their methods. (All the sources at least agreed that vampires are too strong and fast for standard escape and evasion tactics.)

This description got me nowhere so I decided to unpack more of my books. But I still kept thinking about Rafael. His beautiful, graceful body—just like my knight. His fangs—so much like every description of a vampire.

I took another shower, using lukewarm water. My body promptly remembered what it had enjoyed the last time I had stood in the small tiled enclosure and my fingers started playing with myself again.

I wondered if Rafael ever did something like this.

Did he truly enjoy women like that blonde? Or did he sometimes pleasure himself, if only for some quiet?

I called myself names and tried to think of other things, like grant applications for research money or examining an eagle.

But I kept trying to imagine what Rafael would look like if he fondled himself. Would he look ecstatic or pained? Or both? Would he move with style, like the way he'd handled that woman? Or would he be direct? Would he prefer to touch just the shaft of his cock or someplace else?

I climaxed, and found myself waking up to cold water. Again.

June 3

After trying to avoid the subject by doing more unpacking, I finally faced the pile of vampire books and my notes again. My analysis still left me with more questions than I'd started with and I decided to go back into the research center to use their library. I wanted to compare more of the standard literature on predators' physiology to what I'd found on vampires.

My mind was a thousand miles away when I walked into the center just before sunset. I stopped dead when I came into the reception area.

Bob was talking to Rafael.

I froze. All I could think of were his fangs—and the more lurid vampire stories I'd just read, of throats being ripped out and blood spraying the walls and worse. I must have turned white as a sheet. I wished I were carrying my sawed-off shotgun or my Colt which my godfather had given me for protection from rogue animals.

Bob greeted me with a big grin on his face and made introductions, emphasizing that Rafael Perez manages the neighboring land. I must have said something polite, because neither of them seemed surprised by my behavior, but I don't remember.

I suspect Bob thought my silence meant I was sexually attracted to Rafael. He said something about needing to get home now and asked me to give Rafael a private tour.

Bob was out of the building within minutes, before I could refuse or manage a private warning about vampires. Not that he'd have paid attention to either, given his scientific brain and his longing to explore Rafael's land.

Rafael very politely talked about my research as we went through the center. But I was extremely wary of him until I saw him around the convalescent birds. Very few people know how to move around injured wild birds, since you have to be much quieter than most people are used to. But he was as calm as a professional falconer and the birds were remarkably relaxed.

I became calmer the longer I saw the birds' comfort with him. Slowly I started thinking more about my patients and research, less about bloodsucking monsters.

We finished up in the lounge, drinking soda from the vending machine. No sign of bodyguards for him tonight but that was not a subject I wanted to think about. I was just glad to see him drink something other than blood.

Rafael seemed genuinely interested in my dissertation. I talked more to him about it than I ever have to anyone who wasn't on my advisory committee.

It was almost midnight when he truly startled me. "Do you have any questions for me, *querida*?"

My eyes narrowed when he called me darling. Was he coming on to me again? What did he want from me?

"Relax, please, *doctora*. I give endearments only to very special people, not passing fancies. You are a very unique woman," he offered with a slight bow. "I would like to study you, as you would like to study me."

I flushed with embarrassment at being so obvious but felt a chill of fear at the same time. My fingers twitched, wishing for the security of my missing guns.

Rafael stayed perfectly still on the other side of the

lounge from me. He was obviously being very careful not to frighten me.

"How do I know that?" he asked rhetorically. "You saw me last night with the blonde. You have obviously satisfied yourself, *querida*, that she wasn't harmed or you wouldn't be sitting here so calmly with me. Correct?"

I nodded. I've never had a conversation with a predator before and I couldn't have moved to save my life. I didn't know whether I should treat him as a man or as a sexual predator.

"So, what would you like to ask me, *querida*? I believe that the lady was content with the encounter last night."

"Yes, it seemed like symbiosis to me," I said, finding comfort in an academic term. I couldn't believe that I was talking to him about this. "She gets an orgasm and you get some blood. But it didn't look like what the books say."

He smiled at that, a genuine grin with white teeth flashing against his olive skin. No sign of his fangs though.

"Oh, most of the books are very wrong, *doctora*. A few have some elements of truth though." His eyes gleamed at me, with laughter and admiration, I think.

I took a sip of my soda, relaxing a bit more when he showed no signs of attacking me.

"So here you are, interviewing a *vampiro*," he remarked. "An unexpected event for both of us. I will answer your questions, *doctora*, as much as I can. It is a pleasure to converse with a beautiful, intelligent woman." He inclined his head to me while he lifted his soda can, as if toasting me. I smiled back and raised my soda can in salute to him, before trying to fill the gaps in my analysis.

I questioned him for a long time about vampire biology and I'll write up my notes later. Finally I was curled up on that lumpy sofa, finishing the last sentence, while Rafael leaned against the wall.

"I've never before discussed *vampiros* with anyone who wasn't a *vampiro* or considering becoming one. This has been very enlightening for me." He twirled his soda can in those elegant brown fingers. "But you still have one particular question for me, *doctora*. It has been burning your tongue all evening as you start to voice it, then quickly change your words. Do you believe now that I will be truthful with you? Come, ask your question."

I swallowed hard and then asked him that most embarrassing of all questions. "Do you masturbate?"

His jaw dropped and he choked on a mouthful of soda. I blushed and started to say something more, give him an easy exit from answering me. But he closed his eyes and chuckled. My blush deepened and I stayed silent, unable to smoothly change the subject.

His eyes opened, still laughing, and he crossed the room to me. He dropped to his knees in front of me. I stared at him, shocked. He bent his head to me and kissed my hand.

I couldn't have said anything if I'd tried.

"You are truly the most incredible woman. So intelligent and so attractive." He kissed my hand again but more slowly. I could feel his lips move against my skin in a delicate caress. He rubbed his cheek against my hand for an instant and then looked up at me.

"*Sí*, I masturbate but very rarely. I am seldom without sexual companions, as you have undoubtedly guessed. But sometimes, *querida*, I fantasize when I am alone and bring myself to a climax."

A jolt of fire lanced through my body at the images those words evoked. I reached out, very tentatively, and pushed a strand of hair back from his forehead. It was incredibly soft and sleek, curling through my fingers like silk. His eyelids drooped at the contact and his head tilted a little. It reminded me of stroking a bird's head, pleasure and wariness at the same time.

I slid my fingers through his hair again, enjoying the feel. He closed his eyes and gave himself up to my touch, visibly enjoying himself. I petted him a few more times before taking my hand away. I wanted to touch more of him but wasn't sure what to do next.

"Would you like to watch me, Grania?" he asked, his voice a soft rumble in the quiet room.

I swallowed hard, hungry at the thought but unable to answer.

"I think it would bring you pleasure if you watched," he murmured, and I nodded silently in acknowledgment.

"But I would like to ask a favor of you in return."

I eyed him suspiciously, some of my eagerness fading.

"If watching me excites you, may I have a drop of your blood afterward? That would allow me a taste of your emotion, which is what I truly desire, Grania. I swear to you that you would be in no danger."

I thought about it and agreed. He could have killed me at any time during the tour, if he had wanted to. But he hadn't, so maybe he would keep his word. If he didn't keep his word, well, I'd be dead whether I agreed to this or not. "*Sí*, Rafael, you may have a sample of my blood. I put my faith in your honor."

Strong emotion swept over Rafael's face at my words. Surprise? Relief? Joy?

He kissed my hand and stood up. He stretched like a dancer and swayed a bit, then stroked his chest. I blinked when his nipples hardened under the touch. Then he sat down and took his boots off, with a joke about how he appreciated them more at other times. He took his socks off too and spent a little time rubbing his feet.

Somehow his unself-conscious ease with his own body really affected me. I was a little flushed and my own nipples hardened.

Then he stood up again. He turned slowly in front of me, caressing himself and allowing me to watch every angle of his swaying body. He didn't let me get a clear look at his front, only showing me side views or quick turns, as he excited himself. I saw his massive chest rise and fall more strongly as he became excited.

He rubbed and plucked his nipples through the thin T-shirt. Then he slid his hands down over his hips to fondle his rear, which thrust his chest toward me for a clearer view.

I think I gasped. I know I was breathing hard by the time his T-shirt came off.

Rafael's chest and back were deeply scarred. Some of the injuries must have been life-threatening, both whip scars and deep gouges. I shuddered at the pain he must have felt. Then I recovered myself and wondered if he had needed to adjust his hunting technique for those wounds.

But I uttered no questions. I was much more interested in watching a beautiful man enjoying himself. I started to feel damp between my legs. I grew wetter as he rubbed his crotch through his jeans, then fanned his fingers to emphasize his erection. I stayed still though, except for a few wriggles, not wanting to lose control of myself completely.

He took a long time handling himself. My body wanted to attack him by the time he finally unzipped his jeans. His cock was huge. I've seen so few adult men's fully erect cocks but surely Rafael's was unusually large. I was shocked at its size and hungry for it at the same time.

His hand closed around it and he turned partly away from me. The teasing movement inflamed me. He played with himself more and I could see his cock lengthening under the attention.

I cursed under my breath and sat up straighter, needing to see more.

Then Rafael turned back to me. His hand slid inside his jeans and cupped his scrotum. I watched the subtle movements, riveted in place. He played with himself longer before sliding his jeans slowly, oh so slowly, down his legs. Again he teased me by turning so I first saw his buttocks, then his hips and legs, before seeing his arousal in profile. Damn, how I wanted it! I gripped the sofa arm hard.

At last Rafael displayed himself to me proudly, his eyes locked on me. I watched his every move, sweating when his fist lingered at the tip, swallowing when he cupped his testicles. Soon I was breathing when he did, our lungs working in unison as he slowly built our excitement.

His hand started to pump faster and faster. He tried to avoid that, by changing hands and tempo. Pain showed in his face as he fought his own body's demands. But finally his orgasm overwhelmed him. He growled like a wolf as he shot a rich stream of white.

Rafael's legs buckled under him and he sank to his knees in front of me. I reached out to break his fall and caught his shoulders, steadying him. His proud head drooped as he tried to catch his breath. I caressed his hair, crooning to him. But I too was gasping for breath, wishing for my own finish. I couldn't seem to find it on my own.

His head came around under my hand and his mouth caught the inside of my wrist. I relaxed a bit, expecting another kiss. He sucked my skin hard, exactly on my pulse point. I gulped, caught by surprise and a wave of hunger. Then he bit down, hard and clean.

His fangs tied us together as he tapped my blood. The bond transformed pleasure into raw delight, blazing through me like the flame from a welder's torch. I cried out, as fire raced through me and centered deep within me. The orgasm burst through me in a series of shockwaves, tsunamis of feeling that consumed every cell and every thought.

But the aftermath, what the French call *le petit mort*, was different from anything I'd ever felt before. Where

I'd always before been separate somehow from my lover no matter how closely joined our bodies were, this time I felt him somehow in my mind, part of me as I was part of him, ecstasy roaring through both of our bodies and minds together.

It was a long time before I could think again. I found myself on his lap with my face buried against his chest. He smelled of sandalwood, sweat, and sex. His heartbeat, like mine, was a little irregular. I was bitterly sorry in that moment to lose the connection we'd felt as my blood flowed into him.

June 10

Rafael and I ran together this morning. We spoke more about vampires, as he promised. I have promised in return never to speak to anyone else about him. My journal is encrypted now and he has permitted me this record at least.

I must try to retain a professional distance while studying him as a unique predator. I need to limit this relationship to friendship so he won't distract me from my plans.

I can't let myself see him as a man lest I lose control again. He's simply too attractive to me. I've spent too many years, working my way out of the orphanages and gaining my education, planning for children and a good home. I can't throw it all away on a vampire.

But sometimes, when I try to fall asleep at night, I remember how it felt to be joined with him in blood and passion. And I wonder what it would feel like to have that splendid cock buried deep within me.

Then I dream of being his lover and sharing joy with him again.

Author's Note

Grania and Rafael's love story is told in *Bond of Blood* by Diane Whiteside, the first volume of the Texas Vampires trilogy, coming Fall 2006 from Berkley.